D1598649

MURDER
of a
BROTHER

Jack
Crosswell

MURDER
of a
BROTHER

Pentland Press Inc.
www.pentlandpressusa.com

PUBLISHED BY PENTLAND PRESS, INC.
5122 Bur Oak Circle, Raleigh, North Carolina 27612
United States of America
919-782-0281

ISBN 1-57197-265-X
Library of Congress Control Number: 00-135746

Printed in the United States of America

Dedicated to Daphne, my wife.

CHAPTER
One

I was sleeping soundly when the voice on the answering machine woke me.

"Frank, if you're there, pick up," Gloria Walters said urgently.

Oh shit, I thought as I fumbled to snatch the receiver from its cradle and switch off the machine. "What's up?"

"I know it's your day off, but. . . ."

"Why wake me in the middle of the night?" I said.

"It's ten minutes past nine." Gloria, the oldest female deputy in our part of Southwestern Virginia, wouldn't have called unless it was important. "Really hate to—"

"Don't tell me another deer hunter is lost," I said.

"Not this time. There's been a murder. Somebody found a body on the old Rowan farm. The sheriff says it looks like a shooting."

"A shooting?"

"An anonymous caller tipped us off."

"Anyone identified the victim?"

"The boss thinks his name is Joe Sacks."

"Sacks?"

"You know him?"

"Yeah, I know him," I said. Her words hit me in the gut. Sacks and I had done recon patrols together in Vietnam.

"Got the call a couple of hours ago. The man had to be a local to know the Rowan place."

"Yeah," I said. "It's deserted now."

A few years earlier, Deputy Frosty Johnson and I blew up a whiskey still there. I'd punched holes in the dynamite with a screwdriver and threaded the fuses through the perforations. We'd forgotten to bring crimpers, and I bit the caps with my teeth to fasten them on the fuses. After lighting up, I dropped the sawdust-like sticks into the mash barrels and yelled, "Fire in the hole."

The explosions had left mash dripping from the treetops and hazy blue smoke wallowing close to the ground. One shot didn't go, and I waded back into the muddy mess to finish the job. The fumes had given me one hell of a headache—one that I could still remember.

"Where did the call come from?" I asked.

"The computer traced it to a pay phone across from the Apex Shirt Factory. He hung up before I could question him."

"Save me a printout," I said. The Rowan place was ten miles from town and I wondered what the caller had been doing there. "Why didn't you call sooner?"

"The sheriff took the call. He was over at Maggie's Kitchen drinking coffee."

"Who's at the scene now?"

"Sheriff Riggins took two reserves with him. I don't know who from Maggie's followed them out there. Wants you to come pronto and bring your evidence kit."

"Have you notified the coroner?"

"Can't find him. He's not answering his phone, and the hospital can't locate him either. But he'll get to see it on the evening news."

"On the evening news?"

"The TV station at Roanoke is sending a crew. So's the *Roanoke Times*."

"Who in the hell—?"

"Don't even ask," she said. "You already know."

"Okay, I'll be there soon as I get dressed."

It didn't take a genius to figure out that my boss, Sheriff Adam Riggins, had called the press. With an election year approaching, he sucked up media exposure like a sponge. And lucky for him this was Sunday, probably a dull news day. He'd likely make headlines come Monday morning.

"Drive carefully because the roads are slick," she said.

I looked out a window and saw that the season's first snow had fallen during the night. Dark elephant clouds were retreating over the mountaintops.

"My cruiser isn't four-wheel-drive, but I'll get there," I said.

Mostly, I serve civil papers, mainly mundane stuff that keeps the system running for the lawyers. But Gloria's reminder to take an evidence kit wasn't necessary. I jump at a chance to use what I learned long ago as a Charlotte city cop.

I brushed hot lather on my face and shaved with a twice-used blade. I ran a comb through my unruly red hair and brushed my teeth with baking soda. When I finished, I retrieved the car keys from the uniform I'd tossed across the back of a chair the previous night. Barefooted and in my drawers, I dashed outside on the fresh snow and started the car so the engine could warm while I dressed. Rummaging through a pile of grungy laundry next to the washing machine, I found my insulated coveralls.

The heater had cleared the windshield when I stuffed my six-foot-four, two-hundred-pound frame into the driver's seat and pushed the accelerator gently enough to move forward without spinning. My gravel driveway stretches a quarter mile down to a paved public road, which I hoped the state had plowed. I knew I'd be okay once I hit Highway 21. The DOT crews spread chemicals to melt snow on the major routes, but those of us in the back country have to manage on our own.

Billows of smoke spiraling from farmhouse chimneys saved the countryside from being totally bleak as I drove south. Wintry winds had stripped the last leaves off most of the trees, revealing gnarled limbs. These skeletons lined the dual-lane asphalt highway, which weeks ago had been teeming with tourists admiring our fall colors. Then, waving blades of orchard grass had danced with the breezes on fields now blanketed with bone-white snow. The leaf peepers were long gone.

The hunters had now invaded Ottway County's 650 square miles to shoot deer that meander down from the mountains to nibble on hay put out for cattle. But inevitably, somebody gets lost in the Mt. Rogers National Forest, which we patrol under a government contract.

I'd just spent three days trudging through the brambles looking for a hunter. His buddy reported him missing when he didn't return to camp. The state police sent a helicopter, and a Boy Scout troop from a local church helped us search. I finally located the lost pilgrim in a Burnsville motel, shacked up with his buddy's wife. I didn't tell his buddy.

I wheeled off Highway 21 at Farm View Road. Then I drove through a mixture of snow and mud on a gravel stretch for less than a mile. A cement cattle guard marked the entrance to the Rowan place, where fat Angus cattle once grazed before the Rowan family filed for bankruptcy. Now the farm was abandoned and loggers had stripped the big timber, leaving underbrush and multiflora roses to claim the rolling fields. I drove over the cattle guard and followed tire tracks to the edge of a pine thicket, where I saw a dozen pickups parked, along with the sheriff's Cherokee.

Riggins, I saw, hadn't secured the crime scene. He and his followers were clumped around a smoldering fire made from a heap of fallen limbs. Their brogans and cowboy boots had stomped the red mud and snow into mush, impairing my chances of getting physical evidence. I left the plaster of paris in the trunk, grabbing my evidence kit and my Canon A-I camera.

"Got here late, didn't you?" somebody yelled at me. I ignored him.

An unlit cigar jutted from the corner of Riggins's mouth. He and his two reserve deputies stared as I approached. Their fresh tan uniforms told me they hadn't dirtied themselves doing scout work. Riggins was busy politicking.

The gold star glittered on his chest, and his belly overlapped a wide belt that was in its last notch. Along with his britches, the belt held up a ring of keys and a holstered pearl-handled .44 Magnum.

"Stark," said Riggins, "it took you long enough to get here."

"Should've called sooner," I replied.

He took in a deep breath and exhaled. "Where's your uniform?"

"At home. I came to do a crime scene."

"The media is coming," he said. "You'd make my department look better if you'd have worn your uniform."

"So? You don't give me a dry-cleaning allowance. I'm gonna be on my hands and knees digging in the dirt. Where's the body?"

"The EMTs took it to town. Too cold to wait for the coroner."

"Who made a positive ID?"

"Don't recollect for sure," he said. "The dead man is Joe Sacks. Didn't have any identification, but one of the EMT guys remembered him from high school. Did you know him?"

"Yeah, he'd given me information," I said quietly. "And I served with him in the army. We were friends."

"He was a snitch?"

"He was an honest citizen who gave me good information."

"Any idea who'd kill him?"

"No," I said. "If he was on to something, he hadn't shared it with me."

Reserve Deputy Tiny Holly, a telephone installer with a yellow mustache, said, "I used to see him buying wine in town."

I motioned Riggins aside, away from the crowd's earshot.

"Somebody brought him here," I said quietly. "Joe didn't own a car."

"Did he have a record?"

"Nope. Only a public drunk charge or two. He was an alcoholic who squeezed by on a veteran's disability check."

"If he's a veteran, the VFW and Legion boys will want an arrest," Riggins said.

"Where was he when you got here?"

"On his belly right there," he said, pointing to a slick place on the ground. "His hands were tied behind him with bailing twine. And the blood on the front of his jacket had turned black. The EMTs think he was shot in the chest." I saw impressions next to the slick spot and figured it was where they'd set the stretcher.

Deputy Holly and some of the spectators were inching closer, but Riggins was talking loud enough for everybody to hear.

"Did he have a pulse?"

"I don't know," said Riggins. "Didn't wanna touch no dead man. I pushed his body with my boot and there was no life left. He was stiff as a board."

"That meant his body was frozen," I said. "Rigor mortis sets and leaves within forty-eight hours." The dark stains told me that Joe had been dead for two or three days.

"How was he dressed?"

"In an old army jacket and jeans. I remember he had on dirty sneakers."

Joe wore a khaki jacket the last time I saw him—about a week or so earlier at Sheppard's Store. Then, he'd pointed to a faded 82nd Airborne Division shoulder patch. "Remember jump school at Benning?"

I'd nodded. My knees throbbed every day from landing hard in the older chutes that the army has since replaced.

"When he was in high school, Joe pitched a no-hitter that gave Burnsville its only state championship," I said.

"Then this is gonna be a high-profile case," the sheriff said. "Never had anything like this before. If you bust somebody, it'll get me a lot of votes."

Joe had shown me his Masonic apron, but I didn't mention this because of the eavesdroppers who formed a circle around us.

"Anybody been to Joe's cabin?" I asked Riggins.

"No. I don't know where it is."

"When I leave, I'll go for a look. It's near Horse Heaven Mountain. Want to come along?"

He shook his head. "I'll stay and handle the press."

Before I took pictures, I had to ask some bystanders to move from where the body had laid. They didn't budge until I yelled cuss words that put their asses in gear. I shot a roll of Kodak 400 color film, while Riggins apologized for my language. After I finished, I put the camera in its case and snapped it shut.

Then I squatted and sifted through the mud and snow with a metal spoon from the evidence kit. I bagged and tagged chunks of soil for the lab to study. A soil saturation test could tell how much blood Joe lost there. Scrapings from Joe's shoes could be matched with the soil, which might tell if the murder had occurred elsewhere. With no eyewitnesses, I needed all the data I could find.

A TV news crew arrived as I was leaving. A spectator sidled up to my cruiser while I was putting the evidence inside. "If I'm in any of your pictures, make me a copy," he said. "Be nice to hang it on my den wall. I've already got one of me shaking hands with Dale Earnhardt at the Bristol racetrack."

"You asshole," I said. "A man has been murdered and you want a picture?"

His face flushed, and I knew he'd complain to Riggins.

I left the Rowan farm and steered my cruiser south after I entered Highway 21. The snow was slowly melting, and a wind was dusting it from the treetops. I expected the roads to be worse in the Huckleberry Section because of its remoteness. The DOT crews would have it last on their priority list.

CHAPTER
Two

I wouldn't need a warrant to search Joe's cabin since it was now abandoned property, and his privacy was beyond breaching. He'd lived as a recluse communing with nature and the wild animals sharing his hideaway.

"Got a girlfriend?" I'd asked Joe.

"Long time ago I did," he'd said. "She didn't wait."

I keyed the mike twice on the car's hundred-watt Motorola. By breaking the squelch first, I'd snap Gloria's attention from her morning crossword and not have to repeat myself. Something I learned from old Frosty Johnson.

"I'll be ten-six in the Huckleberry Section," I said. "Anybody else working?"

"Just you and the sheriff," she answered. "Nobody's on the air but you two."

I'd guessed right about the roads. The state plows hadn't cleared Old Train Lane and my cruiser began slipping in the slush. But I found some truck tire ruts and let my wheels fall into them. Twisting downward into a ravine, the road followed an old Shawnee trading path for ten miles before rejoining Highway 21. Ahead was the landscape named Horse Heaven Mountain, cold, forbidding, and using up a lot of the skyline.

I let the ruts guide me and hoped that I wouldn't slide into a white-water creek that ran parallel to the road. Joe's cabin, nestled under a tall oak with widespread limbs, was about a hundred yards from Old Train Lane. The solitude reminded me of my boyhood home, a clapboard sharecropper's house with a roof peaked just enough to keep the snow from gathering.

Joe's driveway was too slick to navigate, so I turned around and parked on the shoulder. I looked and listened before getting out. Nothing had changed, it seemed, since my last visit a month earlier. Then his shaggy black dog had run up to my cruiser and challenged me with a growl. This time she wasn't in sight, and I didn't hear her bark.

The place was deserted, but I wasn't going to be deceived by the tranquillity of the scene. I removed my Walther .380 from the glove compartment, stuck it in my side pocket, and picked up my three-cell flashlight. Then I eased the car door shut.

A red fox squirrel chirped and ran up the big oak, shaking his bushy tail at me. He disappeared among the wilted leaves still clinging to the tree. As I trudged ahead, I flushed a family of crows from the ground near the front steps. I read this as a sign that nobody was outside or the critters wouldn't have been there.

My twelve-gauge shotgun would have comforted me more than the .380 with its seven brass cartridges, but I'd left it at home. At close range it's impossible to miss with a shotgun, especially one loaded with No. 4 shot.

I could see tire tracks under the snow leading up Joe's driveway. They weren't fresh, but I couldn't be sure that someone wasn't at the cabin. Whoever left them hadn't been Joe's friend, I figured. I drew the Walther from my pocket and clutched it nervously in my right hand.

Even the shadows were deceptive as I crunched cautiously ahead with measured steps. Joe's dog lay dead at his front steps with a gaping hole in her head. The crows I'd flushed had been pecking meat from her body. The same bastard who'd killed Joe shot his dog, I figured.

"Pup, they play for keeps," I whispered to the dog.

I stepped onto the porch and found the front door unlocked, so I pushed it open and slipped inside with my Walther in the firing position. The house was a darkened hush, and I raised the window shades for light. A previous intruder had ransacked the place, leaving open drawers and red mud caked on the faded linoleum floor. The smell of moldy pintos and stale cigarettes penetrated the air, reminding me that Joe was a smoker. Since there were no bloodstains, I figured Joe had been killed elsewhere.

The timbers under the linoleum creaked when I tiptoed across the room. Chills ran up my spine and I gripped the pistol tighter. I paused, listened, and waited for prolonged moments before moving ahead. A sagging lounge chair sat in the middle of the room, and discarded newspapers cluttered the floor. Except for the squeaking floor, the cabin was quiet. I eased open the back door and faced two outbuildings covered with rusty tin.

There were no fresh tracks, and I approached the larger shed still holding the Walther in my right hand. This had been Joe's wood house, I discovered, and yellow straw covered its floor. It had a dank smell that came from the remnants of gnawed animal bones. Apparently, the dog had also used it as her sleeping quarters.

The second building was a two-hole johnny house, roughly nailed together with pine slabs. Its hinges groaned when I jerked open the door open and looked inside. It was stocked with mail-order catalogs.

I pocketed the pistol and returned to the cabin. An empty wine jug and a large water glass sat by Joe's iron-frame bed. I went through his ransacked dresser drawers and found them surprisingly neat. They contained the usual stuff—clean underwear, socks, and shirts. Joe's medical discharge, Purple Heart, and mail from the VA were in an opened footlocker next to his bed. He'd framed his Silver Star and hung it on the wall. Our captain had recommended him for the Distinguished Service Cross. Joe had traded his pitching arm for the Purple Heart, ending his dreams of playing professional baseball.

No doubt a forensic expert could have done better looking for clues. Riggins, I knew, wouldn't ask the state police for help, so I kept searching. I opened a cabinet and saw Joe's stash of pintos and a half-empty bag of Purina Dog Chow. A Ramon's calendar was next to his stove with a check mark on December 3. A framed picture of Joe in his high school baseball uniform sat on his dresser. He was much younger then, with eager eyes. He looked more like the raw recruit who'd walked with me on recon patrols.

Before I left, I respectfully tucked Joe's army papers, medals, and mail into an envelope. I removed his lodge apron beneath the mattress and took it for his burial. The honorable discharge would get him a VA grave marker and a resting place among the honored. I also took the calendar with the third of December checked. It might mean something later.

I discovered boot prints outside under the eaves where the snow hadn't reached. Whoever made them had an enormous foot, too big for Joe's. Joe was smallish, no taller than five-eight, and Riggins said he'd been wearing sneakers. One thing I knew—this wasn't a routine breaking and entering.

I wandered out to my cruiser and removed a short-handled spade from the trunk. After I scraped away the snow, I attempted to dig a grave in the frozen ground. I managed to carve a shallow hole in which I gently laid the dog, and covered her with rocks. Although it's Mother Nature's way, I didn't want the crows pecking at her bones. She'd been Joe's friend.

Two hours had passed, and a nippy cold wind was biting my cheeks. A string of black clouds floating over the top of the mountain threatened to drop more snow, so I headed for Burnsville. Maybe Maggie's Kitchen would have a slab of country ham left.

As I drove north and back into populated areas, I noticed Christmas displays decorating rural homes, This reminded me that the season had again sneaked up on me. Like other divorced men, I fight depression in December. Mildred had left me eleven years before, taking Frank Jr., Betty, and Arthur Ray, our three children, and blaming my job and beer-drinking buddies for the breakup. All I had from the marriage was a family photo and child support payments. I'd taken scissors and trimmed her out of the photo before hanging it on my bedroom wall.

CHAPTER
Three

Dr. Lincoln Lee, the coroner, shares the basement at Community Hospital with the medical records department, housekeeping, and a single-room morgue.

Just inside Burnsville's town limits, the hospital and its hundred beds sit on a hill overlooking a row of satellite medical and dental clinics. Its parking lot always seems to be full as it was Monday when I parked my cruiser there.

I pushed through the front glass doors, marched straight past the receptionist's desk, nodded to the pink lady on duty, continued past the elevator, and went down a narrow corridor to the stairs leading to the basement.

Doc Lee, clad in a green scrub suit, was dropping coins in a Coke machine at the bottom of the stairs. He snapped open a can, sipped his drink, and motioned for me to follow him to his office. He smiled at a tall woman carrying a stack of charts to the medical records department. She smiled back. The overhead fluorescent lighting illuminated his waxy bald head, giving it a bluish tinge.

He isn't board-certified as a forensic pathologist, but he's all we have. "You're too late for the autopsy," he said.

"I figured as much," I said. "But I had a court case and couldn't get here sooner."

I followed him down the hall and past the medical records department where I heard the clicks of word processors grinding out reports.

"Why'd they move the body?" Doc asked when we got to his office. "The law says you don't do that without my permission."

"Gloria tried to find you. Said she called everywhere she thought you'd be."

"I was teaching Sunday school. You should've known that."

"Yeah," I said. "I was the only kid wearing patched overalls to St. Mark's and you're the only teetotalling Episcopalian I've ever met."

He took a deep breath and exhaled. Then he sat and pointed me to a chair across from him. "Wish I could've examined the body at the site."

"The sheriff was running things."

"The body was in your district, wasn't it?"

"Yes, but Riggins is the boss."

"A bullet in the chest killed Sacks. Powder burns on his skin, close range."

"It was cold-blooded murder."

"Had to be. Whoever shot him damned sure wanted him dead."

"What else?"

"Not much," he said. "No needle tracks—he wasn't an addict. By the bruises on his face, I'd say that somebody struck him several times, but the gunshot took his life. No doubt he was dead when they dumped his body. We'll let the state ME give us more details, if there are any."

"How long had he been dead?"

"Three or four days."

"That's it?"

"Not quite. I think the bullet was a hollow point. It fragmented when it hit his sternum. I recovered some slivers. Maybe a .38 or .357. And I saved blood scrapings for a DNA match."

"Got enough fragments for groove marks?"

"Perhaps. We can try, and hope the State Lab comes up with something."

Before he was coroner, Doc had practiced family medicine until government auditors accused him of overcharging Medicare, which a judge ruled was due to bad bookkeeping and not fraud. During the polio epidemic in the early fifties, he'd worked nonstop for days without compensation. On another occasion, he'd removed a man's appendix on a kitchen table because the family didn't have money for hospital care.

"I've boxed up his clothing," said Doc. "The lab techs may get some fiber to analyze. If you find a suspect, take a sample of the carpet from his car trunk."

"Hell, I know to do that."

He dumped the contents of an envelope holding the bullet fragments onto his desk. Then he then handed me tweezers so I could examine the bits of lead, which I looked at and carefully returned to the desk.

"Got any idea who killed him?" Doc asked.

"No, but they shot his dog and ransacked his cabin."

"This is a case I want solved."

"Did you know him?"

"Delivered him at birth. His parents were my patients, and I was the one who advised him to join the army. As an old army surgeon, I believed in doing duty. Wish I'd told him to run to Canada. By now he would have had a presidential pardon and maybe a World Series ring. He could throw a baseball."

"I was with him in Vietnam," I said without elaborating.

"Then you knew he was a man of character."

"Yeah," I said. "Does he have relatives that you know of?"

"No. There wasn't anybody close. If he had kin, they didn't come to his parents' funerals. I was a pallbearer at both."

I climbed the stairs to the main floor and nodded again to the pink lady as I left. She was reading a book and didn't look up.

CHAPTER
Four

The afternoon sun was turning the frozen stuff into slush when I came from the hospital, and an outside thermometer showed the mercury had climbed to forty degrees. It was almost pleasant as I walked to the parking lot. A catspaw breeze tickled my neck, and I loosened my tie and unbuttoned my collar. Riggins detested unbuttoned collars and loosened ties. His fetish for neatness, I figured, was a hangup from having been a barber for twenty years before he got elected sheriff.

"Come to the office right away," Gloria radioed when I went ten-eight. "The sheriff wants you."

I wasn't surprised because he was worse than my nagging ex-wife had been—always plaguing me for this or that. The pleasure of his absence, I realized, was about to end.

On the way to the courthouse, I wondered why the man who'd reported the murder didn't identify himself. Maybe he just didn't want to get involved, I figured. My Timex showed it was three-fifteen, so I pushed the gas pedal. I'd have to hustle to get my evidence mailed to the state lab before the post office closed at five.

Riggins pays me an extra fifty dollars a month to do paperwork and send stat reports to Richmond. I figured that was what Gloria's call was about. Ten years before he'd hired me to write a procedure manual, and I'd discovered how to get state and federal grants by filling out blank forms. Riggins had jumped at the chance to fill his coffers with free money and put me on the payroll.

I nosed the cruiser into a space reserved for police cars only, got out and walked up a flight of stairs to our office on the second floor. The courthouse was a stone structure in the middle of town that had survived the Civil War. It had a tower on top with a four-way clock that didn't keep time.

Gloria was at her desk when I got to the office. Her robust hips overlapped the chair and she clutched a pencil between her teeth. She was concentrating on her crossword and didn't hear me enter. So I said, "Boo."

She swiveled her head and blinked at me through thick glasses. "Damn you." Slamming the dictionary on her desk, she pointed at a closed door leading to the sheriff's private office. "He's meeting with the commonwealth attorney."

"So?"

"I told him you'd gone to interview Doc, but he's upset. He wants your report on the murder case now."

"Guess what? I haven't done one yet."

"Explain that to him."

"You're a sweetheart," I said. "If you were under ninety, I'd marry you."

"Wouldn't have you, not if you won the state lottery. You're a grouch who goes around startling old women."

Riggins sat slouched in a padded black leather chair behind his desk, chewing an unlit cigar. Hokie Preston, the commonwealth attorney, was across from him in a straight--back chair with his dark wingtips propped on the desk. Hokie's white sideburns and kindly pink face made him appear milder than I'd seen him in court.

"Want me?" I said.

"Where have you been?" Riggins leaned forward and rested his elbows on his mahogany executive desk. "Might try answering your radio." His double chin quivered and his jowls shook like butterscotch pudding.

"Been talking to the coroner."

"You pissed off a bunch of my supporters yesterday."

"What are you talking about?"

"The way you hollered at those people I invited to the scene. Don't you know they vote? Without votes we'd be unemployed."

"I just moved them so I could take pictures."

"You didn't have to be insulting."

"They had no business there," I said. "You should have roped off the area and kept spectators away."

"I'm the boss. Don't tell me what to do. Wish you'd remember this is a small county, and not the Charlotte Police Department. Your temper got you fired there. These citizens you fussed at pay your salary." He scratched his nose with his beefy finger. "Hokie wants you to fill him in on what you've found out."

I shrugged. "So far, I don't know much. No suspects and no motives. Doc says Sacks got shot at close range and that his body was likely dumped later."

Hokie shook his head. "Sounds like you've got plenty of work to do. I just stopped to offer whatever assistance I can give."

Riggins frowned. "Get me a report on what you've got so far."

Before I could answer, Hokie pushed himself out of his chair and cleared his throat. "If you two will excuse me, I'll be on my way." And he sauntered out.

When he'd closed the door, Riggins turned to me. "Let's get the rules straight right now. I'm handling the news media, and I don't want you or anybody else in my department making statements."

"Okay." I waited for the other shoe to drop.

"You've got a smart-ass way of talking and I don't want you fucking up my good relations with the news people. Understand?"

"Get off my back," I said. "You know I don't hand out news releases. And you ought to know the media doesn't give a damn about Joe Sacks or us catching who killed him. They're here to stir up excitement for an audience."

"There's that smart talk I warned you about." By then he was breathing hard. "Put a report on my desk this afternoon."

"Got to ship the evidence by registered mail to the state lab."

"You'll get my report first or else."

As I left his office, Gloria was waiting with a printout of Sunday's 911 call reporting the murder. "It's four o'clock," she said, "but I'll stay if you need me." Our 911 system switches over to the town's police dispatchers when she leaves, and they field our calls. To repay them, we answer town complaints when their cops are busy.

"No thanks," I said. "Got any suggestions?"

"Nary a one." She waddled out of the office carrying a large gray pocketbook that I knew contained a five-shot .38 Chief's Special. "I'm on my way to play contract rummy with the girls."

The printout showed the call was made at 7:15 A.M. from a pay phone across from the Apex Shirt Factory on the east side of town. I wondered if anyone had been working at Apex Sunday morning. I grabbed a telephone directory and thumbed through the yellow pages until I came to the Apex factory. It listed the plant manager as George Brewbaker and gave me his number. When I called his office, he'd already left for the day.

"Would you like to make an appointment?" his secretary said.

"No thanks. When do you expect him back?"

"He's usually here by eight, but he won't see you without an appointment."

"Thank you for your time," I said and hung up.

Riggins passed my desk on his way out. "Don't forget that report. It'd better be on my desk first thing in the morning. And cut off the lights when you leave."

"I'll get your report after I box up my evidence," I called after him.

I scribbled with a ballpoint pen on a yellow legal pad. Then I rolled a sheet of paper into an ancient Underwood in the corner and began typing. With a few strikeovers, I gave Riggins a report that wouldn't have passed freshman English, but he wouldn't know the difference. It took me another hour to prepare the evidence for shipping. By the time I was done, the post office had closed.

CHAPTER
Five

They call Burnsville's east side the Bottom because it's a reclaimed swamp next to the New River. It covers a half-dozen blocks of subsidized shotgun houses thrown up with government loans designed to make a profit for the builders.

Annually during the spring flood, when the New River's brown water jumps its banks, emergency crews evacuate the welfare recipients who live there. Only the Apex Shirt Factory and a bootleg joint known as Good Time Charlie's sit high enough to escape the rampage.

To reach the Apex Shirt Factory, I turned down Pine Avenue, a narrow street with ragged pavement and a pox of potholes. I don't know how the street got its name since there isn't a pine tree in sight. I pulled into the employees' parking lot at Apex, radioed the office of my location, and went into the building.

At five minutes past eight on Tuesday, I faced Apex's receptionist, a sagging, frizzy-haired woman of about forty. She stopped filing her nails when she saw my uniform, and worry wrinkles stretched across her narrow forehead. She put away the file, pushed her chair back, stood, and tightened her lips before speaking.

"Does my son have another speeding ticket? He's been grounded for a month and last night was the first time I let him use the car."

"I'm not here about your son," I said gently. Her expression changed and she quickly regained her composure. Again she was guarding Buckingham Palace. "Is Mr. Brewbaker here?"

"Do you have an appointment?" She knew that I didn't.

"No ma'am, I don't. Tell his secretary it's police business."

"What is your name?"

"Frank Stark, like on my nameplate."

"I'm his secretary," she said. "At Apex most of us do double duties."

The machines made loud humming noises that almost drowned her voice. Their vibrations rattled windows set too high to let the sewing operators peep outside. But I didn't suppose the employees complained, because the plant hadn't moved to Mexico.

"If he'll see me," I said, "it'll keep me from coming back with a court order." I figured she wouldn't know I couldn't get a court order just to interview someone on a hunch.

She picked up her phone and said something I couldn't hear. In less than a minute, a man with beetling dark eyebrows emerged through a door. He stared at me as if he was deciding whether or not to call the company lawyer before saying hello. He decided to say hello.

"I'm George Brewbaker. How can I help you?" He was about forty-five, my age, but was dressed much neater in a gray business suit.

"Need to talk to you a couple of minutes about who was working Sunday."

Brewbaker showed his polished teeth and shot me a corporate smile. "Come this way." His crisp accent wasn't native. He seated me in his office, a twenty-by-twenty room enclosed by sheetrock walls. Behind his desk was a triple row of built-in bookshelves, cluttered with trade journals and textile manuals. A folded copy of the *Wall Street Journal* was prominently displayed on his desk, along with a golf trophy from the country club.

"How may I help you?" He lowered himself into a chair behind his desk and across from me.

"Was anybody working here last Sunday?"

He gave me a puzzled stare. "Is it against the law to work on Sunday?"

"No. Not to my knowledge. I'm not here to arrest you. I want to know if anybody was here Sunday morning."

"Why do you want to know that?"

"I was hoping you could tell me and I wouldn't have to call your corporate headquarters."

His face stiffened and he took a deep breath. "That won't be necessary." Brewbaker slid open a desk drawer and pulled out a stack of time sheets. He put on drug-store reading glasses, licked his thumb, and began riffling through them. "You're not trying to nail us for a labor or safety violation, are you?"

"No sir. I'm investigating a murder."

"A murder?" He looked up and his mouth hung open. "Do you suspect one of our employees?"

"Mr. Brewbaker, right now I suspect every person in Ottway County except myself."

He fixed his eyes on the time sheets and shook his head. "Nothing here. The plant was closed, but one of our fixers could have come in to repair a machine. If he did, he didn't punch the time clock. I have no record of anybody working."

"But you're not certain that a fixer didn't work?"

"No," he said. "Ten people other than me have keys, including three fixers. My family and I were out of town visiting friends, so I can't say nobody was here. Sometimes fixers work off the clock. At six-fifty an hour, they can afford to."

I thanked him, pushed out of my chair, and started to leave.

He held up a finger to stop me. "We make things other than shirts. Right now we're filling orders for men's underwear for a large discount chain. You've probably seen the advertisements on TV. Here, take a pair of our rose-flowered print shorts. They're big sellers this Christmas."

I shook my head. "No thanks. Don't wear rose-flowered shorts." I remembered the itchy ones my aunt had made from chickenfeed sacks after my mother died. While other kids had been playing, I'd been scratching my butt.

After I left Apex, I decided to visit Good Time Charlie while I was in the Bottom. Good Time sold red liquor mostly to customers who stopped by after hours. He escaped the wrath of the law by snitching on crooks. Nothing happened, it seemed, that he didn't hear about, and he had helped me break cases more than once. His two-story house was easy to spot because of the junk cars in his front yard.

"Good Time," I once asked him, "why don't you clean up this mess?"

"If I did," he'd said, "I wouldn't have nowhere to hide my juice."

I climbed the rickety plank stairs leading up to his wide front porch and knocked twice on his door. I didn't hear any movement inside, so I knocked again, this time loud enough to rouse the whole house. From inside came movements—a door creaking open and footsteps. Good Time pulled back a window curtain and peeped out. He opened the door and his dark eyes scanned the front yard. "Don't see no more police, so I don't reckon it's a raid." Good Time blinked at me with the suspicion black people reserve for white men wearing badges.

"It's no raid," I told him. "Need to know what you've heard about a murder in the Huckleberry Section."

"You talking about Joe Sacks?"

"Yeah, did you know him?"

"Remember seeing him pitch baseball. He and my boy were on the same team. Beat everybody that year. Joe threw a left-handed curveball that nobody could hit."

"What have you heard?"

"Only what I picked up on the scanner and read in the newspapers. Nobody is talking much about it. Must've been done by strangers, or I'd have heard somebody say something."

"Much white liquor is coming into town?"

"Damned little. There's a dude selling shine out of his gas station on Highway 21, I hear."

"Where's he getting it?"

"Toby Martin is supposed to be running off some pretty good stuff. He wanted me to take six cases a week but I told him no. I buy mine at the ABC store and resell it. Paying taxes on it keeps the heat off my back."

"Think Toby killed Joe?"

"Could have. He's mean enough, but I ain't heard nothing about him having trouble with anybody lately. Why do you think he done it?"

"Just guessing mostly. Toby's hog farm is only a few miles from where Joe lived. He could have happened up on Toby's liquor operation."

"You need more than that."

"I know. We got the call reporting Joe's death at seven-fifteen Sunday morning. The caller used that telephone booth up the street in front of the shirt factory. Who'd be out that early on Sunday?"

"Lord, I don't know," Good Time said. "My grandson was riding his bicycle delivering the *Roanoke Times*. He's in school now but when he gets home I'll ask him if he saw anybody. Ain't much happens that boy don't notice."

"I'll be in touch," I said. "But I really need help."

"Okay, but don't come back this evening. You'll scare off what few customers I get nowadays. When this county got liquor by the drink, it just about put me out of business, and I'm thinking of letting the junk man buy my wrecks."

"Don't lie to me," I said. "Those junkers are your trademark. Your customers would rather be in your kitchen than sipping cocktails at the country club."

Good Time smiled.

As I left the Bottom, I thought about Toby Martin's rap sheet—three or four assault convictions and more charges that were dropped after witnesses refused to testify. Five years earlier, his wife turned up at the hospital beaten to a pulp. At first, she accused him, but later recanted, and the charges were dismissed.

En route to the office, I stopped at a convenience store bounded by a battery of newspaper racks. I dropped two quarters into a slot for a copy of the *Burnsville Express*, a semiweekly that prints ho-hum fluff. Its streamer headline caught my attention but the account was no more than a rewrite from Monday's *Roanoke Times*. Shitty journalism, I thought.

"You had a call," Gloria told me at the office. "A Miss Tina Jordan left a number for you about thirty minutes ago."

"Who is she?"

"Works for an environmental research group, she said."

I shrugged. "If she inspected my trailer, I'm in trouble. Didn't wash my coffee pot this morning."

"Says she's from Blacksburg. Probably some egghead at the university."

"I'll find out what she wants."

"She's using an office at the County Health Department. It's a local number."

I tried the number Gloria gave me but got a busy signal. Then my brain switched to more pressing matters. What I'd learned about the murder wouldn't fill the inside of a matchbook cover. Calling the Jordan woman could wait. I told Gloria that I was heading toward Horse Heaven Mountain in the Huckleberry Section.

"Thought you'd already checked that out," she said.

"I'm going to Sheppard's General Store."

"You can kill two birds with one stone. Elijah Sheppard called this morning and wanted to see a deputy right away."

"What a coincidence," I said. "He must've heard something about Sacks's murder."

Gloria shook her head. "That's not why that tightwad called. Somebody broke into his outdoor Coke machine and stole twenty dollars. To hear him, you'd think they'd cleaned out Fort Knox."

"Okay, I'll investigate his theft, and he can tell me when Joe last picked up his mail. Elijah meddles in everyone's business, so he just might know something."

Gloria called after me as I was walking out. "The boss wants another progress report in the morning."

"Where is he now?" I said.

"Gone deer hunting with Conrad DeWitte."

"DeWitte is supposed to give a lecture at our lodge tonight." My eyes slipped past Gloria to the wall clock, and it reminded me that I'd have to hurry to be back in time for the meeting.

"The sheriff had me transfer your civil papers to Frosty, but Frosty doesn't know it yet."

As she spoke, I heard Frosty Johnson coming down the hall. His cacophonous laughter bounced off the walls, and I figured he'd told a joke to the county administrator's secretary. Most women found Frosty offensive, but the county administrator's secretary tolerated his raw sense of humor.

"Frank," Frosty said as he came into the office, "you've got a real doozy on your hands, ain't you?"

I nodded. "At least it breaks the monotony of serving subpoenas."

"What do you mean by that?"

"You'll see." I fought to keep from grinning.

Frosty's true name was Fred, and he'd been a deputy under the former sheriff. His nickname came from a full head of white hair that always appeared neatly combed. He was past sixty but still had a finely chiseled face with only a hint of a sagging jawline. His belly was beginning to soften from too much food at Maggie's.

I hurried out before he discovered the papers that Gloria had stuffed in his basket.

CHAPTER
Six

Forty-five minutes later, I arrived at Sheppard's General Store, the last fourth-class post office in the county. I parked my cruiser away from the gas pumps and got out. The store's three stories had been built from heart pine snaked from virgin forests. In the late 1800s, it was headquarters for the now-defunct Eagle Rock Iron and Coal Company. Then the railroad hauled coal and iron ore from Old Train Lane to steel mills in Pittsburgh.

Elijah had finished sorting the morning mail and was griping to a customer about a rural carrier's tardiness when I came in. He gave me an irritated look and handed the customer a roll of stamps. As the customer walked out, he pointed to an antique railroad clock on the wall above his front counter. "It's time you got here."

"What's your problem?" I said.

His green froggy eyes peered at me through wire-rim glasses bridging his curved nose. "What's my problem? I called your office first thing this morning. Expected a deputy before now."

"Here I am."

"Some bastard tore open my drink machine out front and stole the cash box." He came from behind the counter causing his belly to bounce beneath his stripped black apron. He led me outside and I inspected the damage.

"Looks like they used a crowbar," I said.

"Take fingerprints or do something," Elijah said. "I pay taxes and I want protection. Why didn't you come sooner?"

"Came soon as I heard about it."

"Woulda put birdshot in the bastard's ass if I'd caught him stealing my money."

I shook my head. "You can't take the law into your own hands."

Inside, I recognized the handful of old-timers hovering around a wood stove in the middle of the store. They were the regulars, mostly retirees too old for farming chores, but needing a place to discuss world events. I saw them winking at each other as Elijah ranted about the ancestry of the person who'd stolen his money. My visit would be community gossip by nightfall.

"Got somewhere we can talk in private?"

"My office," Elijah said. I followed him down a narrow corridor that winded around a maze of shelves bulging with goods ranging from canned food to motor oil. I ducked to avoid butting my head on merchandise suspended from overhead cross beams. His office was a plasterboard cubicle at the back of the store.

"You've heard that somebody killed Joe Sacks?" I said.

"Yeah." He wiped his nose with the back of his hand.

"Need to ask you some questions."

"Don't know anything to tell you," he said. "Thought you came to catch whoever broke into my drink machine."

"We'll handle that later. When was the last time you saw Joe?"

He scratched the top of his head. "Don't know, but it's been several days."

"When did he pick up his mail last?"

Elijah scowled. "What's this got to do with catching the bastard who tore up my drink machine?"

"Please answer my questions. When did he last get his mail?"

"He hasn't for awhile. His government check is in his box now."

"Do you remember how long it's been there?"

"Sure I do. Since the third. Government checks always come on the third unless it's a holiday or something. If they come earlier, we're not allowed to put them in the boxes until then."

"Was he normally prompt in picking it up?"

"Like clockwork. Wanted it soon as possible so he could buy wine. He wasn't nothing but a neighborhood drunk. If he could hitch a ride, he'd buy his wine at the supermarkets in town. They're cheaper than me. Thought he might be sick or something when he didn't show on the third."

"That helps." Now I knew why Joe had marked the third on the Ramon's calendar.

"He owed me money," Elijah said. "Let him have dog food and pintos on credit. Should have known better. Wine was what he wanted, but I told him he'd have to pay cash for that or I'd get in trouble with the law."

"One thing's sure," I said. "He won't need anymore wine or dog food. Whoever killed him also shot his dog,"

"Who'd want to kill him?"

"I came here to ask you that."

"Don't ask me."

"How much sugar you been selling Toby Martin?"

Elijah was silent for a moment and toyed with the question before answering. "That's none of your business. It's not against the law to sell sugar."

"Might be. You could get caught up in a conspiracy case."

Elijah's voice got squeaky. "Don't you dare threaten me. I'll call Adam Riggins and he'll have your ass. I swing a lot of votes. You'd better be hunting down the bastard who robbed me."

I smiled and a puzzled look wrinkled his face. "The Hatch Act says you feds don't swing votes. And you wouldn't want the ATF and ABC boys checking your files for sugar sales, would you?"

Fire danced in his eyes and he snatched off his glasses. "What do you mean by that?"

"If I called the ATF, Adam Riggins couldn't stop their heat. Wouldn't you rather deal with me than them?"

"Let me tell you, I don't react to threats. You're threatening me, and I don't like it one damned bit."

"If they convicted you of a felony, you'd lose your post office and no telling what else would happen."

He pursed his lips. "I've never had trouble with the law. I'm a respectable citizen. This post office has been ours since my grandfather bought this building from the Eagle Rock company. What could they do to me?"

I shrugged. "You can't predict judges and juries. You could be in big trouble. Every court session, some first offender goes off to prison."

"I'm not a criminal."

"Hope not," I said. "Prove it by cooperating a little. Unless you help me, I might not be able to save you."

"Okay, but it has to be confidential."

"Only you, me, and the Lord above will know."

"What do you want to know?"

"How much sugar is Toby Martin buying?"

He hesitated. "You don't understand. Toby is meaner than the devil. He'll burn down my store."

"Nobody will know unless you tell."

"Okay," he said. "He gets a thousand pounds in hundred-pound bags every week or so. Usually gets it on Sunday mornings before first light."

"Who comes with him?"

"Some longhaired guy who walks with a limp. Toby calls him Dink. I don't know his last name. Ain't from around here."

"Are they picking up half-gallon Mason jars, too?"

"No. I tried to sell him some I had left over from the canning season. Said gallon plastic jugs were lighter and easier to handle. All I'm selling him is sugar. Don't tell anybody I told you this. Don't want trouble with Toby Martin."

"You've got my word," I said. "Do you reckon Martin was involved in Joe's murder?"

"Don't know nothing about that. If Sacks made him mad, Toby's mean enough to kill him. And you'd better watch your backside. Even Toby's family is afraid of him.

Saw him knock his son down for overfilling a gas can. That's why I sell him sugar. I'm afraid not to."

I didn't swallow that line at all. Elijah sold the sugar because he loved money. When an ice storm knocked out electric power for two weeks, he'd milked his customers by doubling the price on his gasoline generators. I'd also heard he loaned money to migrant apple pickers for 25 percent interest.

As I left, I promised to file a report on the break-in so he could collect from his insurance company.

Elijah had corroborated what Good Time Charlie told me. Martin had a whiskey still, probably on his hog farm. It was somewhere he could drive to with a truck. That would explain the hundred-pound bags. Nobody in his right mind would tote hundred-pound bags very far.

I got back in time for my lodge meeting. Riggins was among the brothers seated around a polished oak floor in the red brick building. He was wearing his mirrored tan Tony Lama boots with heels making him taller than his five-seven. He nodded in agreement as Conrad DeWitte, the state deputy grand master, lectured on keeping our morals above reproach.

As chairman of the Ottway County Board of Supervisors, DeWitte was generous with law enforcement—never cutting our budget. He was comely in his blue blazer with brass buttons and gray trousers. His salt-and-pepper hair was neat enough to be a hair piece. For a man of sixty, he was in damned good shape.

He motioned me aside when the lodge had closed. "The sheriff says this poor Sacks fellow was a member of this lodge."

"He was," I said. "I recovered his apron."

"Don't remember seeing him here."

"I don't guess he'd been to the lodge since you moved to Burnsville."

"Do your best to bring his killer to justice," said DeWitte.

"I'm doing my best, sir," I said. "Right now I'm at loose ends. As to who did it, your guess is as good as mine. Joe didn't have any enemies that I can find."

"I'm posting a thousand-dollar reward. No questions asked. For a brother, it's the least I can do. Brothers standing together are strong like a bundle of sticks. As chairman, I'm going to ask the board of supervisors to add to the reward."

Riggins joined us. "Has Conrad told you he's putting up a reward?"

"Yes, and it might help."

"Nothing is more final than murder," DeWitte said. "A person who takes a life steals something he can't give back."

I shrugged.

"Did you find out anything about Elijah Sheppard's drink box?" asked Riggins.

"I talked with him about it. He'll be satisfied if his insurance company pays him for the damages."

As I drove home, I thought about the lodge and Mozart. Some say he wrote his Magic Flute to the cadence of a lodge meeting. I wondered whether or not DeWitte ever listened to Mozart. I didn't, because my music is bluegrass.

Back at my trailer, I checked the blinking light on the machine. Good Time Charlie had called. "Don't call me," he said. "I'll phone you later. Got something you want to know." He never gives his name but I recognize his voice. There was another call from Tina Jordan, the environmentalist at the health department. Said she'd contact me the next day at the sheriff's office if I were available. She sounded sexy.

After I zapped a frozen fish dinner in the microwave, I poured a mule's ear full of Jim Beam in a glass and gulped it down. I chased it with water like a true kitchen sink drinker. I wanted to feel it hit bottom.

The liquor made me nostalgic, and I brooded about Joe Sacks. I could see him clambering up the bunker in the

Quang Tri Valley near Khe Sanh. By himself, he repelled a predawn attack and kept firing, even after they'd shot his arm half off. That memory filled my eyes. I also thought about the dog he loved lying dead at his cabin. Somebody was going to pay for this, I promised myself.

CHAPTER
Seven

"You're late," Gloria told me when I got to the office the next morning.

I looked at my Timex and scowled at her. "What do you mean late? It's only eight-thirty. Can't I stop for breakfast?"

"Didn't mean you're late for work," she said. "You missed Tina Jordan's phone call. Said she'd get back in touch when she returned from Blacksburg."

"Did she say what she wanted?"

"Nope." Gloria shook her head. "Just needed to talk to you. Said she'd call later when she gets back."

I sat at my desk, leaned back in the chair, and interlaced my fingers behind my head. "I won't wait for her call. Somebody must've told her how handsome I am."

"Don't flatter yourself. But get that busted snout fixed and you'd look better. Now you look like a cross between a greyhound and a bulldog."

I rubbed my dented nose and recalled the bastard who had butted me in a three-round smoker at Fort Bragg. It was the last time I ever fought under rules laid down by the Marquis of Queensberry.

"Almost forgot to tell you," Gloria said. "You had another call. A man who didn't identify himself wants you to meet him at the Apex parking lot about nine. Said for you not to drive your cruiser."

I nodded. It was Good Time Charlie, I figured, and he'd probably be in his old black Cad with the rattling mufflers and smoking tailpipes. "Where's Riggins?"

"Gone until after lunch. The Daughters of the Confederacy asked him to speak on home security. They're having their monthly meeting at the Holiday Inn and offered him a free meal and a chance to politic. It was a combination he couldn't refuse."

"I promised him a report. Don't have time to do it. Tell him that I'll try to have something by tomorrow."

She frowned. "One day you're going to provoke him into firing you. You know how he is about reports. If he fires you, you'll have to run for sheriff to get another badge."

"Not me," I said. "I owe Riggins, and I need the check to pay child support until my last kid finishes college."

"That man who called sounded excited and you'd better hurry before he gives up on you."

"How about loaning me your wheels? I'll put some gas in the tank."

Gloria picked up her big gray pocketbook and unzipped it. She fumbled inside and then tossed me two keys held together by a paper clip. "Pat the accelerator twice before you mash the starter. She's temperamental."

When I pressed the starter, I found that Gloria wasn't lying. Her old Chevy groaned for thirty seconds before the engine fired. It coughed a few times and quit, forcing me to restart it twice more before it kept running. The sputtering gradually smoothed out once the engine warmed, but I felt a conspicuous skip as the car chugged toward the Bottom.

Good Time sat in his old Cad just outside the Apex parking lot, and rolled down his left front window when I pulled beside him. "We can't talk here. Follow me up the street to the other side of my house. Nobody will pay no 'tension to us there."

We stopped behind an abandoned house a block beyond his place. He opened his door, slid out of his Cad, and did a quick survey prior to getting into Gloria's car. "Can't take no chances on anybody seeing us. I know who was in that phone booth."

"You do?"

"Yeah, my grandson seen him."

"Who was it?"

"Some white dude in a faded blue pickup truck. My grandson noticed because the truck's radiator was steaming, like it had a busted water hose. The right front fender was bashed in, too."

"Did he recognize him?"

Good Time shook his head. "No. He studied the truck more than the man. He's seen the truck before."

"Where?"

"Right where we just was," he said. "At the shirt factory. It's parked there now. Least it was a few minutes ago. You can see it sitting in the back of the lot. Go look, but I ain't going with you. Don't want anybody seeing us together. If I hear anymore, I'll call."

He slipped out of Gloria's car, looked around, and got back into his Cad. He was gone in an instant, leaving me to pat the gas pedal and coax the old Chevy into running.

Going back up Pine Avenue the car bucked and spat until I got to Apex's parking lot and took a gander. The old pickup was there. It was huddled next to a wire fence at the back of the lot. With binoculars, I could have easily read the tag number—but I hadn't brought binoculars and would have to go inside for a better look. I didn't see anybody standing around, so I drove past a Yellow Freight trailer backed up to a loading dock, and got close enough to copy the license number.

The pickup truck looked exactly the way Good Time's grandson had described it with the smashed right front fender. Soon as I could get to the office, I'd ask Gloria to run a ten–twenty-eight on the tag. Knowing the name of the owner would be a start.

I couldn't help but notice the people living in the rundown houses as I drove out of the Bottom. As a boy I'd lived through those hard times. Perhaps Conrad DeWitte could get our lodge to provide Christmas presents for the neighborhood children. I'd ask.

At a self-service station, I pulled up to a low-grade pump and put two dollars worth of gas into Gloria's tank. Her windshield had cat tracks on it so I cleaned it with a sponge provided by the station. She'd check her gas needle, I knew, to see if I'd kept my promise. She loved that car like it was the child she never had.

The tag number, Gloria found, came back to a 1979 Dodge registered to Eugene Leroy Moffitt, Route One, Box Sixty-Seven, Burnsville. The computer said that it wasn't reported stolen. I'd never heard of Moffitt but Route One wasn't in my district. "Keep this between us for the time being," I said to Gloria.

"Does it have to do with the murder?"

"Moffitt may be our Sunday morning caller. I'm gonna talk to him and tape his voice so you can listen, if he denies making the call. Run a background check on both DMV and the NCIC. I don't have a date of birth, but we may get something."

Gloria punched Moffitt's name into the computer and hit the enter key.

"He's got a record," Gloria said. "Two convictions for DUI. His operator's license is now suspended, but he has limited permission to drive from his home to his job. No track record on NCIC. Check with the clerk of circuit court. He may have a local record not registered on NCIC."

"No thanks," I said. "Skeeter Dobson talks too much to his drinking buddies at the country club. Have you ever heard of Moffitt?"

"No. There's a bunch of Moffitts living on Route One. Don't think I know him, but I probably know some of his kin. If he's been in trouble, it doesn't ring a bit. Frosty might know, but he's out serving your civil papers."

"Moffitt's pickup is parked at Apex's," I said. "I'm going to see if he works there. Get Frosty and ask him to meet me. If Moffitt's our man, I want a witness in case he confesses. Wouldn't want it to be just my word against his."

Frosty answered his radio and said he'd meet me shortly at the Apex parking lot. I slid open the middle drawer of my desk, moved some clutter, and found a mini tape recorder, one that I'd bought with my own money. I dropped it in my coat pocket.

"Are you going to check with Hokie Preston?" Gloria said.

"Not yet. Need to hear what Moffitt says first. Might be nothing and again it might be important. I'll call Hokie later if I need to. Too many cooks in the kitchen can spoil the chit'lings."

Before I got away, Skeeter Dobson bounded into our office bringing a bundle of civil papers from the clerk's office. A medium-sized man with short-cropped brown hair, he gave me an enormous empty smile and waved the papers. "These can wait until next month, but I thought I'd bring them early. With Christmas coming up, I didn't figure you guys would have much to do."

"Thanks," I said. "Give them to Gloria so she can sort them out."

"Anything new in the murder case? Everybody is talking about it."

"We're working on it."

"Tell me if something comes up."

"Okay," I lied.

CHAPTER
Eight

Frosty was waiting in his cruiser just inside Apex's gate when I arrived. He'd stuffed a wad of Red Man into his mouth and was wiping brown saliva from his lips. It took him a few seconds of chewing to manipulate the tobacco before he could speak.

"Need some professional help?" he asked.

I nodded. "Only if you can spare the time from serving civil papers."

"Don't be funny. What have you got?"

"Come inside with me and witness an interview. I think the man who found Sacks's body may work here. Ever heard of Eugene Leroy Moffitt?"

Frosty nodded. "Yes, I know him, but he's not the type to kill anybody. He's a wimp who lets his old lady whip his ass."

I shrugged. "According to DMV, he lost his driver's license. No other record showed up."

"You'd get drunk, too, if you had to live with his old lady."

"You know her?"

"Yeah," he said. "She's a cousin. They both work here at Apex. Let me tell you, she probably weighs as much as his pickup truck."

We went in together. Brewbaker's secretary wasn't at her sentry post, so I led Frosty past her desk and down the hallway to Brewbaker's office. As I raised my hand to knock, Brewbaker opened the door and we stood facing each other. "I was just going to lunch," he said. "Can you come back later?"

"Answer a question first. Does Eugene Leroy Moffitt work here?"

He nodded. "Yes, but—"

"We want to talk to him."

"Does it have to do with that murder?"

I shrugged. "Right now, I'm not sure."

Brewbaker turned pale. "God, I hope Moffitt isn't involved. We screen our personnel to keep from hiring troublemakers. It'd be bad publicity if it made the newspapers."

"I'm not a newspaper reporter," I said, "and we're not accusing anybody. At this point, we only want to talk with him."

"I'll get him to the office," Brewbaker said. "He's a fixer on Line Two. You can use my desk while I'm gone to lunch. That way you won't interrupt our production line."

"What kind of employee is he?" I asked Brewbaker.

"Leroy is one of our better workers. If he killed anybody, it'd be out of character for him." He led us into his office, told us to make ourselves at home, and went after Moffitt.

Five minutes later, Brewbaker brought Moffitt into the office and introduced him. Not much over five feet tall, Moffitt was chubby with skin that looked like the inside of a banana. I looked at him and wondered if he fixed the machines making the rose-colored shorts that Brewbaker had offered me.

"We want to talk to him in private," I said.

"That's fine," he said. "I've got a luncheon date that I'm already late for."

After Brewbaker left, Moffitt looked at Frosty and began wringing his hands. "Calm down," I told him. "We know you called the sheriff's office last Sunday morning."

His voice quivered. "I didn't kill that man."

"We're not saying you did."

"Can I sit?"

"Sure," I said, and Frosty slid a chair over to him.

"Is that blue Dodge pickup truck parked outside yours?"

He nodded. "It's mine." He turned toward Frosty. "Mr. Johnson, am I in trouble over not giving my name to that lady?"

Frosty shrugged. "We don't know yet. Answer Deputy Stark's questions, and, by God, you'd better tell him the truth."

"Yes sir. What do you want to know?"

"First, let me read you your rights." I fumbled in my billfold and pulled out a Miranda warning card, which I read slowly with the clearest diction I could muster. "Do you understand what I just read to you?"

"Yes sir. I understand."

"Did you call the sheriff's office Sunday morning?"

He hesitated, looked first at Frosty, and then at me.

Frosty prodded him. "Tell him the truth."

"Yes sir," said Moffitt. "I called."

"Why didn't you give your name?"

"Was scared to get involved. Finding that man was the worst thing I ever seen."

"You'd better level with us," Frosty said.

"Honest to God, I'm telling the truth. My dog found that body while I was rabbit hunting."

"It's against the law to hunt on Sunday," I said. "That can get you in trouble."

He looked at both of us with pleading eyes. "Will you help me if I tell the whole truth?"

"You'd better not lie," Frosty said. "You talk first and we'll see if we can help."

"I didn't kill that man," said Moffitt. "Didn't know who he was until I saw it on TV. Remembered him then. He used to play baseball. Finding him scared me near 'bout to death. Ain't told my wife why I can't sleep at night."

"You were hunting Sunday?" I said.

"No," he said. "Found him Saturday. My beagle was sniffing something and I went to take a look. I saw it was a man's body, lying on his face. I knew he was dead."

"Why didn't you call then?"

"Cause the judge revoked my driver's license. I'm only supposed to drive from home to work. I got limited privileges. Didn't want anybody to know I'd used my truck to go rabbit hunting. The judge told me I'd have to pull time if I drove anywhere but from home to work."

"How old are you?" I said to him.

"Be thirty-eight my next birthday."

"What have you been convicted of?" I said.

"Twice I've been up for driving drunk. That's all." His reached into his shirt pocket with a greasy hand and pulled out a pack of king-sized Chesterfields. "Mr. Johnson will tell you I've never been in trouble with the law."

Frosty nodded. "I believe he's telling the truth."

"Okay if I smoke?" Moffitt asked.

"Help yourself," I said. He used both hands to hold his match steady while he lit up. "What time did you find the body?"

He rolled his eyes toward the ceiling and waited a few seconds before answering. "Must've been around ten. It was before lunch, cause I was too scared to eat when I got home. My wife had cooked chicken and dumplings. She thought I was sick."

"Was there snow on the ground then?" I said.

Moffitt shook his head. "No sir. It didn't snow until late that night."

"Describe exactly what you saw," I said. "Did you see fresh tracks or any signs around the body?"

"I saw where somebody had parked a vehicle, but it wasn't fresh. Could have been a couple days old. I don't remember many details because I was too scared. I got my beagle and went straight home fast as I could. I was afraid that if somebody saw me they'd kill me, too."

"Will you take a polygraph test?"

He raised his eyebrows and looked at Frosty. "A what?"

"A polygraph test," I repeated.

"What's that?"

"It's a lie detector test," Frosty said. "It'll tell us whether or not you're being truthful."

"I'm sorry that I didn't know what that was. I ain't got but a fourth-grade education. I'll take the test anytime you say. Would the judge have to know I drove my pickup to go rabbit hunting?"

"No," I said. "Not if you're telling the truth."

"If I take the test, please don't tell my wife. She'll raise hell and make me get rid of my dog."

"We won't tell her," I said. "But you'd better be telling all you know. How can we get up with you later? Got a home phone?"

"Call me here at the plant," he said. "I'll let Mr. Brewbaker know."

"Contact us if you remember anything else," Frosty said. "If I was you, I wouldn't tell anybody here about our talk."

"Can I go now?" he said.

"Yes," I said, "but remember we may need to talk again."

Frosty and I walked past the receptionist's desk, and the frizzy-haired secretary had returned. She frowned at us, but I smiled and nodded.

Outside, Frosty said, "Are you gonna run him through a polygraph?"

"No," I said. "I mentioned it for a psychological effect."

Frosty nodded. "That man's too scared to lie. I'll see you at the office."

My belly was growling so I stopped at Maggie's, sat at a table near the front, and looked at the street through her plate glass window. She served me a double cheeseburger that I washed down with a mug of black coffee.

Maggie said, "You're investigating that murder case, aren't you?"

"Sure am," I said.

"Joe Sacks used to stop by and I'd fix him a hamburger steak. Sheriff Riggins comes here every morning running his mouth. He couldn't stop talking long enough to listen, even if I knew something to tell him. But I can talk to you."

"Do you know anything?"

"No, but if I hear of something, I'll let you know, not him."

CHAPTER
Nine

"Gonna let Riggins know we found the anonymous caller?" Frosty asked as we walked up the stairs to the sheriff's office.

"No, I want to save Moffitt from a media blitz."

"The boss ain't gonna like that once he finds out."

"I don't want him telling the judge that Moffitt violated his limited driving privileges. We might need him as a witness. Let's keep this part of the investigation secret for now."

Frosty nodded. "You can do what you want. I've got things to do and they don't involve hanging around this office."

He left me with my notes and the old Underwood typewriter. I was pecking away with both of my forefingers when a statuesque brunette entered the sheriff's office. Neither Gloria nor I noticed until she pushed the bell at the service counter, causing Gloria to struggle from her chair and plod across the office. "May I help you?" she said.

"Yes, I'm Tina Jordan and I'm here to see Deputy Stark." Her soft voice complemented her pleasant oval face. I did a quick take and saw a strikingly handsome woman with long dark hair worn loose about her shoulders.

"That's me," I said, rotating in my chair.

"Can we talk in private?"

"Yes," I said, "we can use the sheriff's office."

I nodded her into a seat across from Riggins's desk and seized a rare opportunity to flop down in his armchair. She folded nice long legs. Her apple-sized breasts beneath the pullover sweater didn't escape my notice, and roused more than my curiosity.

"Mr. Stark," she began.

I managed a smile. "Call me Frank. Everyone else does."

"As you may know, I'm doing an environmental study on streams in Southwestern Virginia, particularly in Ottway County. I'm gathering water samples for testing."

"No, I haven't heard about any kind of study."

"Somebody has threatened me."

"How?"

"With an anonymous telephone call."

"What did they say?"

She thought for a moment. "Told me I'd better go somewhere else if I wanted to stay healthy. Didn't want me poking around where it was none of my business."

"Have you called the town police?"

She shook her head. "No, because I've been working out of the town limits near Horse Heaven Mountain in the Huckleberry Section."

"That's my territory."

"They told me so at the health department."

"Why should somebody care about your work?"

"I don't know. I've only taken a few specimens and the results have been negative."

"What are you testing for?"

"To see if any of the old mines are leaching chemicals into the water."

"Those mines closed before World War II," I said. "The people who worked them are long dead."

"I know," she said. "But it wasn't a ghost that threatened me, and I don't think I'm paranoid."

"Not much going on in Huckleberry. Farmers raise a few cattle, and maybe some logging is done, but I don't know anything that would contaminate the streams. Maybe a farmer thought you were going to block him from watering his stock. People are upset because the Soil Conservation Service is talking about fencing off creek banks."

She cocked her brows, and her dark eyes reflected the blue of her sweater. "Runoff caused by logging operations can be devastating."

"Conrad DeWitte owns the only lumber company in the county."

"So?"

"He's chairman of the county board of supervisors and an environmental supporter. I can almost take an oath that he didn't threaten you."

"Well, I haven't been near any livestock. That's not my purpose. We're looking for leachate. Years ago there were no regulations governing mine closures. Mostly, the operators just boarded up the entrances, stopped the pumps, and walked away. Without the pumps, water filled the tunnels. There are microbes that can turn iron ore and sulfide into sulfuric acid. Enough of that could cause a disaster."

I shrugged. She'd gone beyond my chemistry 101 course. "When did you get this call?"

"Monday afternoon. It was a man with a deep voice. It didn't overly concern me until I read in the *Roanoke Times* about that murder. That's in the same general area where I've been working."

"Not exactly," I said. "Joe Sacks was found closer to town."

"Still, it's the same general area."

"What do you know about that homicide? Anything you should be telling me?"

"All I know is what I read in the newspaper."

"Anything make you suspicious?"

"Absolutely nothing." She smiled. "I'm here checking water quality, not solving murders, and I do expect police protection. I've taken this threat seriously."

"Take all threats seriously," I said. "Whether anyone intends to carry them out is another question."

"I'm working under a federal grant. It'd be embarrassing for your department if I had to call upon the

U.S. Marshal's Service for protection. Don't you get federal funding?"

I nodded. "Yeah, half of our budget depends on it. But we don't get enough to be bodyguards for every federal worker who comes through."

"Are you saying I'm wasting time asking you for protection?"

"Not at all. We protect all of our citizens."

"The murdered man didn't sound protected."

I shrugged. "You probably got a crank call that has nothing to do with Joe Sacks's death."

"How did the caller know where to reach me? I wasn't advertising my presence. To my knowledge, nobody saw me wandering around. An old pickup truck passed, but the driver didn't look my way. The little Escort I drive is not the kind of car that attracts attention."

"Lady, I can't—"

"If I can call you Frank, you can call me Tina."

"Okay, Tina. I can't be your bodyguard. We don't have the manpower. It's tough to find enough time to investigate this murder."

She looked at me with unsmiling almond-shaped eyes that were like dark blue pools. "What should I do?"

"Take somebody at the health department with you. Your caller will probably cool it if he sees you're not alone."

"They're shorthanded. Can you loan me a portable radio?"

"Not on your life," I said. "Damned talkies won't work that far out anyhow. When are you going back to Huckleberry?"

She took a deep breath. "In the morning."

"Call me before you leave. If I can arrange it, I'll follow you. That's my best offer."

Her body movements were fluid as she walked out. Not bad—I told myself—not bad at all. She must've known her good looks had gotten to me, or maybe I was daydreaming.

My last stab at romance had been almost a year earlier when Margie Reynolds came to teach home economics at Burnsville High. She was on the rebound from a failed romance, and we hit it off. Or I thought we did. But our fling ended when the school year closed.

"Darling," she'd said one night with her eyes filled, "you're great in bed and I'll miss you. But I don't see anything permanent between us. You're too dedicated to your job. I need to be first, not second to your department."

I didn't know what to say so I remained silent. As she left my trailer, she looked once over her shoulder, and I believe she expected me to call her back. I didn't. Nor did I attempt to contact her later. We had said our good-byes.

"That girl is too young for you," Gloria said when I returned to my desk. "She's in her twenties. You need somebody more mature."

"Nothing there," I said. "That visit was professional. Never saw her before."

"I saw you looking at her. Reminded me of Frosty trying to woo the county administrator's secretary."

"Well, she is damned sexy, " I said. "And I've got a date with her in the morning."

"A date?"

"Yeah, we're going to the Huckleberry Section. Somebody's threatening her."

"Never take up with a woman who's got more problems than you."

"This is official business."

"You're not taking her to Maggie's for supper?"

"If I wine and dine her, it won't be at Maggie's. If she's hungry, I'll feed her biscuits and molasses at my place."

"Biscuits and molasses aren't romantic."

"If she doesn't like biscuits and molasses, she ain't my kind of woman." I handed her my page of strikeovers and asked her to type them neatly for Riggins. Then I left.

CHAPTER
Ten

Frosty was leaving in his cruiser when I arrived at the courthouse the next morning. He pulled back into his parking place and signaled for me to join him. His frown was big enough to have stopped the useless four-way clock atop the courthouse had it been operative.

"What's eating you?" I said. "You don't look happy."

"I'm not happy a damned bit. Riggins chewed my ass out for not telling him I went with you to interview Moffitt. Even snapped at Gloria for working her crossword on county time."

"He knows about Moffitt?"

"Damn right he does, but I didn't tell him. Wanted to know where you were."

"Hope Gloria handed him my report."

"She did. That's why he's raising hell. You didn't mention Moffitt."

I shrugged, got out of his car, and went upstairs. An early-morning ass-chewing would brighten my day. I passed Skeeter Dobson toting a stack of documents from his office to the courtroom. I said, "Hi, Skeeter," but kept going.

As I expected, Riggins ambushed me as soon as I walked through the door. He had been sitting at my desk, but got up and crooked his finger for me to follow him into his office. "Don't let anybody disturb us," he said to Gloria before he slammed his door shut.

"What's the matter?" I said.

"You ask what's the matter? I'm your boss, and I think you're not keeping me up to date on your investigation. Skeeter Dobson says that you're about to arrest the man who killed Sacks. I'm the sheriff and I have to hear this from the clerk of court. He's told everybody in the courthouse, and that makes me look like a fool. Why haven't you told me?"

"What are you talking about?"

Between heavy breaths, Riggins said, "Some guy named George Brewbaker saw Skeeter Dobson at the country club and told him that you might arrest one of his employees for killing Sacks."

"Read your report."

"I did. You don't have anything in it about any suspects."

"I interviewed Eugene Leroy Moffitt, who works for Brewbaker, and he's not a suspect. If he was, you'd be the first to know."

"Then why interview him?"

"To see if he was the person who found the body and called Sunday morning."

"Was he?"

I paused for a moment, scratched my ear, and then told him that he was.

"Damn it," Riggins said. "Tell me every step you take. You're forgetting I'm the boss and I'm the one who hired you. What makes you think Moffitt didn't kill Sacks?"

"Because he's a wimp who couldn't beat his meat without changing hands."

"Have you discussed this with Hokie?"

"No," I said. "No reason to at this time."

"Remember," Riggins said. "Clear things with me before you take any big steps. The ultimate responsibility falls on me."

"I know you're the boss. You often remind me of that."

"Then start taking orders. When you were flat on your ass, I gave you back a badge, don't forget. I hired you after the Charlotte Police Department canned you for being a hothead."

I changed the subject. For ten years I'd lived with the fact that the Charlotte Police Department let me go, all because I'd punched out my ex-wife's second husband for belt whipping one of my kids. He was a city councilman's son, and his broken jaw didn't boost my standings with the department.

"We've got an environmental problem to deal with this morning," I said to Riggins.

He wrinkled his face and peered at me. "What are you talking about?"

"Somebody has threatened an environmental researcher working in the Huckleberry Section. Her name is Tina Jordan."

"That's not our problem."

"She's filed an official complaint with us."

"Does she know who threatened her?"

"No, it was a telephone call."

"Damned environmentalists are ruining the country," he said. "They want to stop farmers from watering their livestock in the creeks. Any farmer could have made that call. Can't much blame them. Has she been trespassing on private property?"

"Said she hadn't been off the state right-of-way. Whoever called knew to reach her at the health department. Who'd know that?"

"It's been in the newspapers. Against my advice, our county board asked for a water study. It's a waste of taxpayers' money, but Conrad DeWitte thinks it's a step into the future."

"She wants me to escort her out to Huckleberry."

"No. We're not getting involved in that mess. The farmers would run us out of the county."

"If we don't, it might cost us," I said.

"How?"

"She knows we get federal funding, and the feds are sponsoring her research. If she has to call the U.S. Marshal's Service for protection, it could cost us our grant money."

I watched Riggins struggle with this. He wasn't about to jeopardize a grant that financed half of our salaries and helped buy new cruisers every two years. And he didn't want federal marshals keeping the peace in his county. He wiggled his unlit cigar and made humming sounds to himself for what seemed like a long time. "I don't want anybody to know we're babysitting a damned environmentalist."

"We need that grant money."

"Puts us smack between a rock and a hard place, all right." Riggins swallowed hard.

"Told her I'd follow when she went to take samples this morning. Shouldn't take much time."

"You'll piss off every farmer in the area," Riggins said. "If they see you riding shotgun for her—no telling what'll happen on election day."

"If we don't go and she's hurt, you can say good-bye to your funding, and the media will eat you alive. So will the taxpayers when they have to make up for the lost financing."

He rubbed his forehead. "Just don't follow her in your cruiser."

"What do you want me to do? Ride a bicycle?"

"Don't be a wiscass. Go in her car."

"You want me to ride with her?"

"Might work if you shuck your uniform. Go home and put on civvies. Maybe nobody will notice. Sit low in the seat and cover your face. When you leave with her, don't look at people and they won't see you."

Riggins abruptly got up and left the office. Soon as he'd cleared the door, I got Tina on the phone. "I'm going, but we'll have to use your car."

"My car?"

"Yeah," I said. "I'll be wearing plain clothes. Meet me in the courthouse parking lot in an hour."

I hurried home, dusted off the dried mud, and changed into the same outfit I'd worn the Sunday we'd found Joe's body. This time I dropped a full box of .38s into my coat pocket.

CHAPTER
Eleven

Within an hour, I arrived at the courthouse and pulled my cruiser next to Tina's yellow Escort wagon. I got out and strode toward her vehicle. She did a double take when she saw me wearing woods clothes.

"I thought you cops always carried guns, but I don't see yours."

"Don't fret," I said. "I'm packing, but I'll give you ten-to-one odds I won't need it."

"I hope you're right," she said. "But I'm glad you're coming with me."

"I've even got binoculars and a talkie stuffed in my game pocket. Only trouble is the handset won't break the squelch where we're going."

After we got underway, she said, "You look younger out of uniform, and not so stern. I almost didn't recognize you. You could pass for Daniel Boone."

"Sheriff Riggins suggested I wear this," I said. "If anybody's after you, he'll come closer to showing himself if I'm incognito." No use saying that Riggins didn't want anyone to associate his department with an environmentalist.

"You don't look very official," she said. "Nobody I know would identify you as an officer of the law."

"Don't poke fun, I'm a pretty sensitive guy."

As we tooled south on Highway 21, I adjusted the rearview mirror on the passenger side, and I didn't see anything suspicious. Behind us was the usual traffic, delivery trucks and a few pickups weighted down with round bales of hay. Two cars and an empty pickup truck passed, but their drivers didn't give us a second glance.

"So far we're not being followed," I said.

"I didn't notice anything out of the ordinary before."

I looked when Tina made a left swing off Highway 21, and nobody turned behind us. She drove a short distance and swung again, this time to the right, and we were on Old Train Lane. I was surprised that her Escort navigated the ruts so well, although she scraped the bottom a few times in the deeper holes. Horse Heaven Mountain and Joe's cabin stood directly ahead. She continued for about two miles and stopped at a one-way bridge, not too far from Joe's cabin.

When we got out, she took a black case of pint-sized glass bottles from the back seat. I said, "Is this where you were working when you got your threat?"

"About a hundred yards behind us closer to the intersection. Does it mean anything?"

"Most of this land is posted. Maybe you went where you weren't supposed to be."

"According to your county map, the state has a forty-foot right-of-way from the center of the road. I didn't go beyond that."

"Maybe somebody thought you did. Why is that mountain so important?"

"Several streams flow out of it. By circling it, I can get a fairly accurate reading on what's in it."

"Horse Heaven Mountain is honeycombed with natural caves and old mine tunnels. Now, it's growing up with brush and trees. For Ottway County, it's like Mount Rainier is to the State of Washington."

"You've been to Washington?"

"For a few months I was at Ft. Lewis," I said. "It's beautiful out there.

"Do you know who owns Horse Heaven Mountain?"

"Some land company in Atlanta, I think. They've plastered posted signs all over. Conrad DeWitte must have a contract with the owners. His company is cutting logs on the other side that comes out on Highway 21."

"Hate to see our forests destroyed."

"DeWitte is an environmentalist," I said. "Far as I know his company abides by the anti-erosion standards the state sets."

"Clean water is what my work is all about."

I nodded. "But I can show you places on the National Forest that loggers left looking like a bombing range."

"How'd this mountain get its name?"

"Old-timers say that Confederates hid their horses here during the Civil War when Yankee patrols rode through. After the Yanks pulled out, the women folks would hang out laundry on their clotheslines. It was a signal telling the Confederates that it was safe to come down. They didn't start mining big-time until the war ended."

"According to this map, there are three bridges on this road."

"Sounds right," I said. "The next one is a converted railroad trestle. It's listed on the state historical register, which means it can't be replaced."

"See the muddy water?" She pointed at the stream beneath the bridge.

"You can't expect it to be clear with this runoff from melting snow."

"No," she said, "that's why it's the best time to collect samples. If there's leachate, the water will pick it up. It's like carbon dating. Tests will show what's been dumped in the watershed for the past hundred years."

She moved toward the creek with an erect carriage that claimed every inch of her six feet. Her hips twisted just enough to be sexy and to hint that her jeans hid a tremendous pair of thighs.

I was leaning against a willow tree and watching when I heard a motor vehicle approaching in the distance. An older model black Dodge van soon came into sight but I wasn't alarmed. I figured a deer hunter was looking for an easy roadside kill. Tina was scooping muck from the creek-bank mire and didn't look up from her work. I concealed myself behind the tree, out of sight from the road, and watched the vehicle move slowly toward us.

The van startled Tina and she looked toward me.

"Just keep taking samples," I said. "Probably somebody passing through. If he isn't, I've got you covered. They haven't seen me."

The driver's face was blurred and I couldn't tell much about him. I grabbed my binoculars and trained them on the van's license plates. Mud had covered the numbers, but I saw that it was a Virginia issue. The van passed Tina's Escort, rounded a curve, and disappeared.

"What was that all about?" Tina had walked nervously over to where I was standing.

"Man apparently wanted a peek at a good-looking woman. You probably took his mind away from his deer hunting. We'll see if he comes back."

She returned to the creek and was almost finished at this site when I heard the van returning, or at least the motor sounded the same. This time it was going faster and I could hear its wheels crunching on the gravel.

"Keep taking your samples," I said. "Maybe I can get a better look when he comes through."

The van shifted down and then stopped in the center of the road. As Tina turned her head, a second man quickly opened the rear door and fired a rifle. She dove behind a rock in the stream, splashing water against the bank, and I hauled out my revolver and shot twice. My bullets thudded against metal as the shooter slammed the door. I looked and saw that Tina was wet, but okay.

The driver revved up and roared off before I could get off another round. I saw the van's wheels spinning and its rear end fishtailing as it vanished. I tried the handset but couldn't trip the relay. Then I waded into the creek to help Tina and saw that she was visibly shaken. I took her hand and we climbed the bank together. Then she pressed her trembling body against mine, and I held her in my arms while she sobbed.

"Are we gonna be all right?" she asked.

"Sure. He's not likely to return. His license plate was covered with mud, and I couldn't get a reading. Might not have helped anyway, because criminals usually run stolen plates."

"He'd have killed me if you hadn't surprised him."

"Don't think so. If he'd wanted, he could have hit you. He had a scope, and I believe he was using a .270. That was a warning. They didn't expect me to be there shooting back."

"Why are they doing this?"

"I don't know, but he wasn't a local farmer."

"How do you know?"

"I'm acquainted with most people in Huckleberry. I've never seen those guys or that vehicle."

"Think they'll come back?"

"Not after the surprise they got," I said. "They'll be long gone by now."

"You don't think they'll be waiting to ambush us?"

"Not a chance." I wasn't that sure, but I didn't want a hysterical woman on my hands. "Can your lab detect spent mash in the water samples?"

"Yes, I suppose so."

"I'm curious to know if there's a whiskey still on that mountain. Once I saw spent mash floating on top of the water in a stream and it was miles from the still. It looked a little bit like soap suds."

"Nothing like that showed up in the specimens I took the other day. But we haven't established a baseline for the toxicities."

"I know, but ask your lab to check it out. Could be a residue in there we can't see. Right now, that's the only explanation I have. Trouble is, I've never known moonshiners to shoot at women."

"Will the state police help?"

"Not unless the sheriff requests it, and you can bet that he won't."

"Why not?"

"Has something to do with guarding his territory."

She slowly pulled herself away from me. "Let's get back to Burnsville," said Tina. "My nerves are shot. Couldn't you feel my heart pounding?"

"Sure could. Have they scared you off?"

She shook her head. "No, but I gotta regroup."

"Let me know before you come back here."

"Do you mind driving my car back to town?"

I nodded and got behind the steering wheel and adjusted the mirrors.

"Tell me about yourself," I said as I headed toward Burnsville.

"What do you want to know? At this moment I'm too shaky to talk."

"Conversation helps relieve tension and brings you back down."

She thought for a moment and said, "There's not much to tell about me. Nothing like this has ever happened before."

"How did you wind up here?"

She hesitated again, and I turned and saw her looking out the window. Finally she said, "Finished my undergraduate work at Wake Forest and came to Tech for my master's. I'm originally from New York. Ever been there?"

"Never," I said. "Uncle Sam sent me to Japan and Vietnam. That's the limit of my travels. I did work for the Charlotte Police Department. Charlotte seemed like a big city to me."

"It's a small town compared to New York."

"Do you miss the bright lights?"

"Not at all. Until I was threatened, my stay has been peaceful. My first job was teaching science, and I even found high school freshmen peaceful."

"Why'd you quit and switch to this job?"

"To help our environment."

"You're not married?" I asked.

"Tried it once but it didn't work out. How about you?"

"Tried it once and it damned sure didn't work. I've been single a long time."

I thought about inviting her to my place for a drink and a TV dinner, but didn't. With her being a New Yorker, I figured she'd be condescending in my paltry surroundings. As we got closer to Burnsville, I tried the talkie, and this time I tripped the relay and got through to the office. I described the van and asked Gloria to put out an alert on the state police channel. "There may be two bullet holes in the vehicle's rear door. Ask the town police to check the emergency room at the hospital in case I got lucky."

Riggins intercepted the transmission on his car radio and was on the air immediately. "What's happened?" The signal from his unit crackled with static and I couldn't understand him.

"I'll be at the courthouse in ten minutes," I replied. "Will explain then."

"Do you need medical attention?" Gloria asked.

"Negative," I told Gloria, "but some hot coffee would help."

Riggins and Hokie Preston were sitting in the sheriff's Cherokee when we got to the parking lot. I don't know how the word got out so quickly but a covey of curious townspeople was clumped there, too. Riggins got out, yanked a fresh cigar from his shirt pocket, and jammed it into his mouth. Hokie walked around the Cherokee and joined him.

"What happened?" Riggins spoke loudly.

I didn't reply but glanced at the civilians. Tina marched through the onlookers and faced Riggins. "Somebody shot at me, and this man saved my life."

"I shot back," I said, "but I don't know if I hit the shooter. That's why I radioed for someone to check the hospital emergency room. Whoever they were, they escaped in that van I described to Gloria."

"I hope you knew what you were doing," said Riggins. "Shoot somebody without justification and we're all in trouble." The spectators were edging closer.

I swallowed hard and stared at him. "Whoever shoots at me buys himself a ticket to hell if I can get him."

Hokie sauntered over to where I was standing and patted my shoulder with his hand. "Sounds like you were justified. When you do your report, burn me a copy for my files." The sun bounced off his pink cheeks and gave his nose a reddish tone. He smiled and tipped his felt hat to Tina. "I'm Hokie Preston, the commonwealth attorney. Hope you get a better impression than this of our county."

"Think I should organize a posse and go to Huckleberry?" Riggins said. "I can call out our reserves."

"Be a waste of time," I said. "Those bastards are long gone. They probably turned south on the hard surface road and headed for the state line. You can notify the North Carolina Highway Patrol."

I took Tina by the arm and coaxed her toward the courthouse entrance. No use broadcasting our business. Riggins followed as I took her upstairs. I grabbed the coffee pot as soon as I got inside the office and filled two plastic cups. I handed one to Tina and sipped on the second one myself. With Riggins looking over my shoulder, I flopped down at my desk and began scribbling notes while my recollections were still fresh.

"Don't leave until you read this." I handed Tina the first page of my notes. "Feel free to add anything that I might have missed."

Riggins moseyed over to Tina's chair. "Ma'am, be sure to tell your people that my department has been cooperating."

"You can count on that," she said. "Deputy Stark saved my life."

"Are you staying in town?" he asked.

"I have a room at the Riverview Inn, about a block from the health department."

"Good place," Riggins said. "Know the owner."

I read Tina's notes and they were as I had expected. She'd only gotten a glimpse of the shooter and probably wouldn't be able to identify him. Like me, she thought he was heavyset and dark. Together, we jotted down our statements, and I handed our scribblings to Gloria for typing. I wasn't up to using the old Underwood.

"You're lucky that Hokie thinks your reaction was justified," Riggins said to me. "After Gloria types your report, I'm showing it to the news people. I'll have a press conference here in the morning."

"Is that wise?" I said.

"Yes. I want the public to know we're doing our job."

"You can tell them the shot didn't come from a local farmer."

Hokie broke his silence and prodded Riggins into ordering a stack of ham biscuits from Maggie's. He also got Gloria to turn up the heat since Tina and I were still damp and feeling chilled.

By four, we had finished reviewing Gloria's typed report, signed it, and gave Riggins a copy. "I'll drive Miss Jordan to the Riverview Inn," Riggins said, "and ask the town police to keep an overnight surveillance on the place."

Tina looked at me and I nodded. "I'll see you in the morning," I told her. "My home phone is listed. Call if anything comes up."

Riggins led her out of the office.

When they'd left, Gloria said, "I warned you that she is too young for you."

"Should have asked her to my trailer for a drink and a TV dinner," I replied. "Maybe you could read some romance in that."

I headed home knowing that the excitement I'd experienced would keep me awake unless I could dull it with strong drink.

CHAPTER
Twelve

I slept for eight hours but I felt worn to a frazzle when I turned back the covers the next morning. Old Sol was peeping over the mountaintops and I should have been raring to go, but the bourbon I'd downed the night before left me with a hangover. Somehow, I managed to pull up the covers and grab a second nap before the telephone woke me.

"We can't let them get away with this," Frosty was yelling over the phone. "Heard about it at Maggie's and I told them it'd take a lowdown skunk to shoot at a woman. Got any idea who it was?"

"No," I said as I fought to get my brain to function. "They were strangers to me."

"I'm breaking out my heavy artillery, and we'll go together to Horse Heaven Mountain. If they want a shootout, we'll give them one they won't forget."

"Okay," I said with a yawn, and agreed to meet him later in the courthouse parking lot. By meeting outside the office, I hoped to avoid Riggins and escape his yak-yak.

After we hung up, I dragged myself into the kitchen and nuked a mug of instant coffee. My brain cells were shouting for caffeine, and I hoped the instant stuff would suffice. I did figure it would be better than warmed-over coffee. Frosty says warmed-over coffee and woke-up women aren't worth the trouble.

I gulped several sips from the mug before my brain started clicking. The man shooting at Tina from the van baffled me, and I became more perplexed when I raked my mind for answers. Without a known motive, I didn't know which way to turn. The shooter could have killed Tina but he didn't. He shot close enough to scare but not injure. I hadn't been much protection, firing my pistol like a novice as the van drove off, and I was still in the dark about Joe's murder. Missing was the key element that would make all of this dovetail together.

Then I began to speculate about Tina. Was there a hidden agenda that I didn't know about? Was there something in her past she hadn't told me? I wondered. She'd mentioned a failed marriage. I've seen jealous spouses do crazy things. Maybe her ex was trying to frighten her into coming home. I'd have to ask her about that. This didn't explain things, but it was the best I could do at the moment.

I drove past Maggie's without stopping. With my head pounding like a bass drum, I'd skip talking to the morning motormouths bunched at the liars' table. They'd be curious about the shooting and I'd let Riggins explain. Perhaps he could decipher the turbulence in Ottway County's peaceful milieu, because I couldn't. When the morning crowd dispersed, I'd get Frosty and we'd go there for some real coffee.

But my luck ran out when Riggins radioed for me to come straight to the sheriff's office. I figured Frosty would hear the traffic and quietly wait for me at Maggie's. Riggins was half smiling and leaning back in his padded chair when I appeared. His hair had been fluffed with a blow dryer, and I remembered that he was expecting the media.

His skin tightened when he saw me, and his attitude changed, turning his face into one big frown. "Beth Sawyer from Channel Three and other reporters are on their way here. Do you have anything to add to your report before I release it?"

"No. Frosty and I are going to Horse Heaven Mountain and see if we can learn anything new."

"Hope you can find something, because your report doesn't have anything to catch the media's eye."

When I checked my basket, I found a message from Tina. She would be at her office at the health department for the day. Nothing else had happened but she didn't sleep well, she'd said. I was glad she didn't ask to go back to Horse Heaven Mountain, but was disappointed that she hadn't called me at home. Perhaps I was reaching for something that wasn't there.

Paul Simmons, editor of the *Burnsville Express*, hobbled into the office before I could grab my stuff and get out. Father Time and a worn-out knee gave him uncertain steps, causing him to lean on a cane and waddle like a duck. He walked past Riggins and Gloria, coming straight to my desk. Without looking up, I could have identified him by the smell of his aftershave. He is the only man I know who pays to have his face lathered and shaved every day in a barber shop.

"Heard about the fun you had." he said. "All I want to hear is who, what, when, where, and why."

"I'll do the talking—" Riggins interrupted.

"You weren't there," Simmons said. "I was listening on my scanner. You were here in town."

I chuckled. When I joined the department, I brought a list of coded signals from Charlotte that would have helped guard the privacy of our radio traffic. Riggins rejected it because he said the codes were too cumbersome.

"He works for me," Riggins said. "I'm the sheriff and he's my deputy, in case you've forgotten."

"You should cooperate," Simmons said. "You'll need me more than that upstate press at election time."

Just the mention of the election got Riggins's attention. He swiveled his head toward me. "Go ahead and tell him."

"Two unidentified white males in a van," I said, "approached and one took a shot at Tina Jordan."

"Is she the woman doing that study on our streams?"

"That's her."

"That's all you know?" the editor said. "You were in a shootout, and that's all you can tell me?"

"Right now that's it," I said. "If I find out who they are, I'll put their asses under the jail, and you can quote me on that."

"And you didn't recognize them?"

"No. Never saw them before that I can recall."

"Do you suppose you hit one of them with your shots?" Simmons asked.

"Don't know. They weren't sociable enough to stick around and chat."

"What were you doing out there?"

"Helping Miss Jordan get water samples," I said. "She'd been threatened and requested assistance. It's all in my report."

"That doesn't mean we're supporting that kind of project," Riggins said. "The federal government doesn't have any business meddling in our county. Frank wasn't getting any samples himself. He was guarding her because of the threats."

"My newspaper supports this study. Our water systems are fragile, and sedimentation from any source can destroy us."

"Don't care," Riggins fumed. "I thought the county made a big mistake by going along with that clean-water business."

"Can I quote you?" Simmons said.

"No," Riggins said. "But I don't want our farmers thinking I'm causing them trouble."

"I hear that the government is going to buy Horse Heaven Mountain," Simmons said.

"First I heard of that," Riggins said. "Don't know why they'd want more land. They can't take care of what they've got now."

"It's nothing I can pin down," he said. "I made some phone calls but nobody official is talking. The district ranger says the Forest Service doesn't really want the land but somebody high up is forcing the sale."

"Doesn't a land company in Atlanta own it?" I asked.

"Yeah," Simmons said, "but it's a dummy corporation. I've tried tracing its true ownership but I get nowhere. According to rumor, a powerful United States senator is a silent partner in the venture. This I can't verify, but I haven't heard anything lately."

"Who's pays the taxes?" I asked. "That's public record."

"Central Land Company of Atlanta," he said. "It has a post office box but no telephone listing. Conrad DeWitte leased the timber rights for the west side of the mountain, but he told me his dealings with the company had been done by mail."

"I've seen his trucks hauling logs from there," I said.

"The land company is probably squeezing out every dime it can before transferring ownership," Simmons said.

"Sacks's cabin could have been on its property." I pointed out the area on a county map hanging on the wall. "It'd be hard to determine without a survey and title search. Land ownership in Huckleberry most often is iffy. The utility companies can't help because they haven't strung lines there."

"Think there's a connection between today's shooting and Joe Sacks's murder?" Simmons asked.

"No," Riggins said. "At first I might have thought so. Not now. Sacks must have been in a drunken brawl, but don't quote me. Degrading a war hero wouldn't look good in print."

"When they arrive, is that what you're telling the state press?" Simmons said. "I don't want you holding out on me."

Riggins's face flushed. Both Simmons and I knew that he liked dancing to the tune of live TV cameras. I also didn't expect him to support me if I got myself into a jam.

"I'm not making an official statement," Riggins said. "And Paul, don't you quote me as saying anything about a drunken brawl. That boy was a decorated veteran, and I'm not stirring up any dirt."

"He was also a lodge brother," I reminded Riggins. "You should respect his memory for that alone." Simmons lifted his eyebrows, and I realized that he wasn't a brother.

Then, he asked, "See any connection between the land owners and Joe?"

"Not likely," I said. "The land company could have easily evicted Joe with a court order. No need to kill him. I'd like to know who's behind the land company but I don't have any evidence that it's involved. Since the pen is mightier than the sword, why don't you dig up a revealing story about the Central Land Company?"

"Don't think I haven't tried," Simmons said. "Can't trace anything beyond the post office box in Atlanta. I've heard another dummy corporation in Boston owns Central Land Company, but I can't verify it. That senator has covered his tracks. Don't have the money it would take to do more than I have."

"Not likely a senator would be connected in Joe's murder," I said.

"Back in the old days," Simmons said, "bootleggers hauled hooch all the way to Chicago from their stills on Horse Heaven Mountain. Reckon moonshine is making a comeback?"

"Not that I know," I said. "People would rather deal dope. It's easier. Making liquor is hard work."

"Forget about that land company," Riggins told me. "So far as we know, it has nothing to do with Joe Sacks. Besides, we don't need trouble with some big-shot senator. Let Paul write what he wants so long as we're not involved."

"Give me the scoop when you figure things out," Simmons said. "I'd hate for the *Roanoke Times* to beat me in my own county."

"I don't see why," I said. "Your original coverage was a *Times* rewrite. You coulda mentioned that he'd been a baseball pitcher at Burnsville High and a war hero. I hope the Lord doesn't judge him by your obit."

Simmons shrugged as I walked out of the office.

CHAPTER
Thirteen

Frosty was sitting alone at the liars' table in the center of Maggie's dining room when I entered. Seeing me, he simultaneously tried smiling and wiping his mouth with a paper napkin. It was a messy attempt that caused him to smear gravy across the end of his nose. I grinned but he didn't. By then the morning regulars had gone, giving me a chance to talk to him in private.

Maggie gave me a smile and strolled up to the table, and she wrote on a pad when I told her I wanted a plate of pancakes and sausage. She then disappeared into the kitchen.

"Glad I came early," Frosty said. "The early bird gets the information."

"What information?"

Frosty shot me a coy smile. "Something you wanna know."

"Quit playing cat-and-mouse."

"I'm not playing cat-and-mouse. I got some information. Good information."

"Are you going to tell me?"

"Sure," he said. "But remember the walls have ears."

I looked around. The place was empty except for Frosty and me. Maggie was in the kitchen frying my pancakes. "There's nobody here."

"Toby Martin has a still," he said in a near whisper.

"Do you know where?"

"No, but he's got somebody delivering shine to the Orange Fix-It Shop on Highway 21."

"Are you talking about that old garage that's been converted into a filling station?"

"That's the place. A man from North Carolina is running it now, and selling the hell out of bootleg whiskey. His name is Marvin Moore."

I winced because the Orange Fix-It Shop is in my district, and I should have been more alert to activities there. Nobody had complained, and I hadn't known about the bootlegging until Good Time Charlie told me. But I didn't mention that to Frosty since you don't identify your snitches. "Did your informant say Toby has a still?"

"Not exactly," Frosty said.

"What do you know about Moore?"

He shrugged. "Not a damned thing except that he's pushing moonshine and selling homegrown grass. My source says the liquor comes every Monday morning before first light."

"Did you get a description of the vehicle?"

"No. But the driver is Pete Dinkins, and I believe he's the same one you caught poaching and shooting deer at night years ago."

"He's the one Joe Sacks reported to me. He and his brother couldn't resist taking a shot at the gleaming eyes of a dummy I'd set up in a field."

"I remember. You hit one so hard he was out cold for an hour."

"They resisted," I said. "While I was cuffing Pete, his brother smacked me on the head with a flashlight. That's when I lowered the boom. Lucky I'm a two-hundred-pounder with a tough skull."

"Old Pete will be surprised to see you again."

"If we can catch him, he might roll over and give us Toby's still."

Maggie stopped our conversation when she shuffled up to the table bringing my pancakes and almost spilling a pitcher of syrup. Before retreating to the kitchen, she refilled our coffee mugs. When she was gone, Frosty said, "You think this liquor operation has anything to do with the Sacks case?"

"Yeah. I'm not sure how. If we can make it hot enough, somebody's bound to talk. Got a hunch Joe walked up on Toby's still and that Toby killed him. But I don't have any proof."

Frosty impatiently drummed his fingers on the tabletop as I finished washing down the pancakes with coffee. "Hurry up. We need to check out Huckleberry so I can get back and serve those papers."

"Let me finish," I said. "I had to wake up with instant coffee."

"You don't understand. I'm dropping my work to help you."

Before he got into my car, he took a World War II–vintage carbine from the trunk of his cruiser. It was, I saw, a Universal model with a 30-shot banana clip. He patted the old gun lovingly and said, "This'll take care of business if anybody wants to monkey with us." He propped the carbine upright between his knees as he sat on my front seat.

"That's your heavy artillery?" I said.

"Yup, paid nine dollars for it at a surplus store. Until now, I've never had a reason to tote it. But I test-fired it before I left home and it shoots good, even if the ammo is old. Hit a tin can dead center at eighty yards."

As we drove south, we passed the Orange Fix-It Shop, which sat on a flat of about two acres between two hills and just west of the highway. Some of its windows were broken and patched with plyboard. It was bounded on every side by a gravel-covered lot that stopped at a garage compartment attached to the rear of the dingy, concrete-block structure. Once it had been bright orange, but the elements had darkened the paint to a reddish purple.

Only three or four vehicles were parked around the gas pumps at the front of the building—nothing suspicious. Two men were standing in front of an old ton-and-a-half Chevy truck with a rusting dump bed. They were looking under its raised hood. No sign of the van. I shifted my eyes

toward Frosty—he was snoozing. Now and then, he would
snort and flip open his eyes.

At Old Train Lane, knobby snow tires had blotted out
the slim prints left yesterday by Tina's Escort. The newer
tracks, I figured, may have been made either by hunters or
curiosity-seekers who monitor our radio frequency. This
was a public road. I pumped the brakes twice and jolted
Frosty from his nap.

"What's up?" He fought to suppress a yawn.

"We're at Old Train Lane and I see fresh tracks."

He patted the carbine's barrel. "I've got ole Betsy ready
in case of trouble."

"I'm not worried," I said. "Most likely hunters came
through."

"Ain't this land posted?"

"Posted signs don't mean much out here."

I drove slowly and looked at the dirty snow banks on
both sides of the road, following the fresh traffic until we
reached Joe's cabin. I stopped and parked on the shoulder
of the road. We got out and trudged toward the house with
Frosty carrying the carbine in the crook of his arm.
Nothing, it seemed, had changed since I'd buried Joe's dog.
I looked at the pile of rocks and the grave was undisturbed.
I found everything as I'd left it inside, and then we
returned to my cruiser. The tracks I'd followed
disappeared on the blacktop at Highway 21.

"Think we ought to go by Sheppard's Store?" Frosty
said.

"Not with what you found out about those liquor
deliveries. Toby lives near there, and I don't want to spook
him in case he drives past."

"Let's do something. I don't have all day to joyride
with that stack of papers to serve."

"Let's take another look at the Orange Fix-It Shop," I
said.

"What are we looking for?"

"A place to hide and catch Pete Dinkins making his drop. Grab him on the ground and we won't have a high-speed chase."

"You're not gonna walk out Toby's farm?"

"Not in this slush. I'd leave too many signs. I want more information about the location of his still before I hike."

Going back to Burnsville, we did a running survey as we passed the Orange Fix-It Shop. The ton-and-a-half Chevy truck was gone, but the other vehicles were still there. I drove just fast enough to keep from being conspicuous while I scanned the woods for a place to conceal the cruiser next Monday. Most trip drivers scouted their drop points before committing themselves. Anything they saw that didn't seem right would cause them to hightail it.

"There's a good path right there." Frosty pointed to a dirt trail across the highway from the filling station.

"Are you sure?"

"I know the place. It deadends at a trash dump where people throw their old refrigerators and washers."

"Some of us really love our environment."

"I've used that path myself," he said, "but not to get rid of trash. Many a sweet thing surrendered to my charms in those woods. The path is solid rock, and nobody will see us from the road."

"We'll have to be in place before sunrise," I told Frosty, knowing that he liked to fill his belly at Maggie's every morning. "You are going to help, aren't you?"

"Since I got the information, I think it's nice that you asked."

CHAPTER
Fourteen

I thought it was my lucky day when Riggins's Cherokee wasn't in its parking place when we got back. Frosty bounced out of my cruiser, saying that he'd be upstairs later. I figured he was going to have his daily prattle with the county administrator's secretary and shook my head.

"I'm back," I said to Gloria, who put down her crossword and peeped at me over her glasses.

"I can see that you are. You just missed Riggins," she said. "He's gone to the Gold Point Section with Billy Bob Perkins to politic."

"It is my lucky day after all," I said, mostly to myself.

"Don't be jealous. Billy Bob is Riggins's nephew and heir apparent to the sheriff's job."

"Believe me, I'm happy that Riggins has gone to Gold Point. It's thirty miles away. That means I can do paperwork without interruptions. Has anybody called me?"

"I'd have told you if they had."

I could see that Gloria was uncomfortable when I ranted about Riggins. She turned away, slid open a file drawer, and made a show of arranging dossiers. And she was suddenly silent.

Frosty broke the silence when he strode into the office and made a beeline for his basket, and picked up a handful of civil papers. "Wish the boss would hire a deputy to do nothing but serve these papers. It'd free me and Frank to do criminal investigations."

"Don't have enough crime for a full-time position, much less two," Gloria said. She picked up her crossword, and without elevating her eyes, she said, "Who was the actor named Robert in the original play, *How to Succeed in Business Without Really Trying?*"

"I don't have any idea," I said.

"That's an easy one." Frosty surprised us both. "It was Robert Morse."

"How'd you know that?" I asked. "Didn't know you were into working crosswords."

"I'm not," he said. "Bobby and I were sonar strikers together in the navy. In Oran, he stood on the fantail of USS Picking and sang to Arabs riding past on camels. It really made those Arabs laugh." Frosty's blue eyes twinkled as he recalled the event.

I shook my head, got up, and went into the sheriff's private office to make a long-distance call.

Ed Creason, the resident agent in charge, answered when I punched in the ATF number in Roanoke. I hoped he'd be able to help catch Pete Dinkins when he dropped off his liquor. The ATF would have good radio equipment with scramblers that the locals couldn't monitor.

"This is Frank Stark." He knew me because I'd made an undercover buy for him over in Franklin County, obtaining two sawed-off shotguns and a fully automatic AK-47.

"What's up?" he said.

"We're planning to bust a moonshine delivery Monday," I said. "Thought you boys might want a piece of the action."

"Are you kidding?"

"No, I'm dead serious."

"They don't let us work moonshine anymore," he said. "Unless there's a bombing, arson, or major firearms violation, we let the locals handle it. Catch a top-ten felon with an Uzi and we may be able to adopt the case."

"Elliot Ness would turn over in his grave."

"Mr. Ness retired before I came on the job."

And then, just as I hung up, I turned to see Conrad DeWitte walking into the office. Gloria gave him her best smile and a musical hello. He was wearing a dark blue suit and a matching vest, not the kind you'd buy at a discount store.

"Need to speak to you and Frosty alone," DeWitte said.

Gloria frowned when he didn't include her, but he disarmed her with a smile that showed his even, white teeth.

"Okay," I said. "Let's use the sheriff's private office." Frosty followed us into the room.

After we'd settled into chairs, DeWitte said, "This morning I told Frosty that a man named Pete Dinkins was delivering moonshine to a place on Highway 21."

"The filling station?" I said.

"Yes, that's the place."

"Frosty told me," I said. "He didn't say the information came from you." I glanced at Frosty and he looked out the window.

DeWitte said, "I've found out this Dinkins drives an old Lincoln and is carrying a gun. He's working for a man named Toby Martin. You'd better be careful dealing with him. He may be involved in your murder case."

"Think you've got the straight poop?" I said.

"One of my employees told me. He stopped at a bootleg joint and saw things."

"Was he there when Dinkins made a delivery?"

"I think he was," DeWitte said. "He drives one of my trucks, and left early last Monday. The roads were icy and he stopped at that place until the plows came through. While he waited, he saw three or four people come in and buy bottles of moonshine. I'm ashamed that he parked a tractor-trailer bearing my logo at a bootleg joint."

"How'd you find out?"

"Through my operations manager. When he told me, you'd better believe I called the driver into my office and chewed him out. It won't happen again."

"Did you fire him?"

"No," DeWitte said. "Would have if he hadn't been truthful. He knows now that I value my reputation."

"He doesn't know you're telling us this?"

"Of course not," DeWitte said. "My operations manager doesn't know, either. Didn't even tell my wife, God bless her."

"Did he say anything that would link Dinkins to Joe Sacks?"

"Not exactly," DeWitte said. "But from what I heard, Joe was buying booze there. As a lodge brother, I'm disappointed that he would have associated with those kind of people."

I laced my hands behind my head and leaned back in Riggins's padded chair. I'd never known Joe to drink anything but wine. There hadn't been any empty whiskey bottles in his cabin when I searched it. "Do you know anybody who saw him there?"

"Offhand, I don't," DeWitte said, "but I'll talk with my employees and see what I can find out. My driver said people at the filling station discussed Sacks, and said that would teach him to sneak up on stills."

"Let me know if you hear anything else," I said.

Gloria knocked on the door. "Frank, you've got a telephone call."

DeWitte pushed himself out of his chair and was gone before I could ask him about helping the welfare kids living in the Bottom. Frosty went to his desk and flopped, grumbling about the stack of papers piled on top.

Tina was on the phone. "Have you found out who shot at me?"

"No, but I'm looking."

"You don't have any new leads?"

"Not a one. Could we talk about it later over a steak and baked spud?"

"At Maggie's?"

"Only if we make it before seven," I said. "Her steaks are good, but she doesn't offer champagne and candlelight."

"Why the seven o'clock deadline? Do her prices go up then?"

"No. At seven she closes and locks the front door."

"Give me a rain check. I'm going to Blacksburg to turn in my reports. The big bosses in Washington aren't going to believe what's happened."

"Don't they watch television?"

"It didn't make the networks, and the local channels don't reach Washington."

"When are you coming back?"

"I'm not sure," she said, "but I'll call. I'm invited to the usual Christmas parties, the kind where a good time is had by all."

After I hung up, Gloria looked at me and shook her head. "Don't be discouraged," she said. "Puck said the course of true love never runs smoothly."

"Who in the hell is Puck?" I didn't tell her that I'd played Bottom in the Bard's *Midsummer Night's Dream* during my high school days.

"If you worked the morning crossword, you'd know," Gloria said. "You should find yourself a plain girl and quit chasing the ones you can't catch."

I shrugged and dropped the department's three handsets in the chargers. When fully charged, they ought to break the relay from the Orange Fix-It Shop. Since the ATF wasn't coming, Frosty and I had the raid to ourselves. None of Riggins's reserves had ever made a bust, and expecting them to help would be like leaning on a straw. I didn't want their inexperience compromising my case. Billy Bob Perkins and the other two paid deputies wouldn't be much assistance either. Billy Bob was the only one under sixty.

CHAPTER
Fifteen

I didn't have a plan so I spent the rest of the week visiting residents in the Huckleberry Section. I must have asked a million questions and fell short of getting the first good clue. Nobody admitted having seen a black van, and all they knew about Joe's murder was what had appeared in the newspapers. I did steer clear of Horse Heaven Mountain and Sheppard's General Store.

To keep Riggins off my back, I supplied him with a ton of meaningless information he could share with the courthouse denizens. I did include a signed statement from a retired judge who had a hunting cabin in Huckleberry. His Honor didn't know anything about the murder, but getting a signed statement from a judge impressed Riggins almost as much as an arrest. He went up and down the courthouse corridors flashing it for show-and-tell.

Tina didn't call again, and I was afraid she'd forgotten the excitement we'd shared on Old Train Lane. The feel of her wet body against mine still excited me. I wanted to pick up my phone and punch in her number. Gloria and my common sense told me that I didn't need the burden of entertaining a charmingly pretty woman, but my heart wished otherwise.

On Friday I beat Gloria to the office and turned the tables on her. I was checking the freshly charged handsets when she waddled through the door and planted her rotund behind in her swivel chair.

"Aren't you a bit late for work?" I said.

She gave me a go-to-hell scowl, and I could almost hear her brain clicking. "Do you always sound so British early in the morning?"

"Only when I want to be as smart as Sherlock Holmes."

"Have you heard from Tina Jordan?"

"She called the other day, but it was all business."

"Frank, act your age. She has her own life away from here, and you might as well accept it."

I wasn't in the mood to hear Gloria's monologue about romantic endeavors, since she was an old maid who didn't even have a house cat.

"When I want advice, I'll write Ann Landers," I said, and went to Maggie's for breakfast.

A blaring noise from the jukebox besieged my soul at Maggie's. Frosty was already seated at the liars' table, and grimacing with pain. He looked at me with pleading eyes while a longhaired youth sat at another table snapping his fingers and patting his foot.

"Teenagers ought to be outlawed," he said. "Can't even hear myself think for that damned noise. Should go over and pull the plug."

"You can't do that. He might file a class-action suit against all the old farts who don't appreciate loud music. Unplugging the machine could suppress a desire and cause him to grow up and be a deputy sheriff."

When the record quit, Frosty took a deep breath and sighed. "Hope that kid doesn't have any more quarters."

"Have you heard a weather report for Monday?" I asked.

"Yeah, it's gonna be cold and windy, but there ain't no snow in the forecast."

"I'll drop off and be on the ground."

He nodded. "Too cold out there for my old bones. Be hard for me to stay warm even with the car engine running."

I'd spotted a high ridge across from the Orange Fix-It Shop, just off the path that Frosty had selected, and figured it was ideally situated for the surveillance. From there I should have a clear view of the target area and the traffic on Highway 21. My camouflaged poncho would make me unobtrusive to passing traffic. This I knew was a one-shot chance that we could blow if we were spotted. We'd have to work under the cover of darkness.

For protection against a slippery start, I bought a box of old-fashioned cat litter so that I could sprinkle it under our wheels in case the path iced up. "Almost good as chains," I explained to Frosty when he saw me with it.

On Monday two hours before daybreak, Frosty backed my cruiser up the wooded lovers' path, and I got out with my down-filled sleeping bag. The Orange Fix-It Shop was dead as a cemetery, and it was too early for much traffic on Highway 21. A tiny slice of yellow moon still hung just above the mountains, but there wasn't a cloud in sight.

Before I could hold the binoculars, I warmed myself in the sleeping bag. My body was shivering so much that I got blurry images when I tried to train them on the target area. Once I thawed and had steady hands, I climbed out of the bag and focused the glasses. I didn't see anybody stirring. An outside mercury light at the station cast eerie shadows that fluttered hauntingly when the wind blew and gave the gravel in the lot a pinkish glow.

The sunrise chased off the moon and the traffic began to flow. First a single car or two passed, and then they came like a string of ants. Some, I figured, were heading to Maggie's for breakfast before going on to their jobs. But I didn't see Dinkins in the traffic.

I had begun to fret about him not coming when the old Lincoln Town Car approached like a queen ant. It bounced like a vehicle riding heavy on Monroe load levelers, and I knew it was carrying juice. The big V-8 talked loudly and popped like a Detroit diesel pulling a semi up a steep mountain road.

Dinkins geared down but didn't stop. He passed the shop and kept going toward town. I adjusted the binoculars and watched his taillights disappear over a hilltop.

"Shit, he drove past without stopping," I whispered to Frosty on the talkie.

"Think he saw something?"

"Don't see how he could."

"Might be making a pass to see if it's clear."

"Yeah," I said. "We'll give him plenty of time."

The minutes passed so slowly that I began to wonder if he was coming back. He could be dropping his booze elsewhere.

In about fifteen minutes, I saw the Lincoln coming back from the direction of town. This time, when Dinkins slowed, he made a deliberate swing into the filling station lot. I heard his tires crunching on the frozen gravel as he drove toward the attached garage at the rear of the building. Since his brake lights didn't flash when he stopped, I figured he had a cutoff switch.

"Let's go now," I radioed Frosty. "He just pulled in." I could see the Lincoln's silhouette behind the building. Frosty revved up and came out spinning, slowing enough for me to dive into the front seat. "Give her the gas," I said. "He's there now."

Frosty stomped on the accelerator and the cruiser leaped forward, fishtailing out of the woods and onto the highway, causing a passing motorist to hit his brakes. We spun onto the filling station lot. Dinkins scrambled around on his front seat and looked our way. Frosty slammed on the brakes and we slid sideways, stopping just short of smashing into the Lincoln. The mercury light reflected on the cars, and I saw Dinkins staring wildly at us. He flung open his car door and hit the ground running. I jumped out to go after him.

Before I could get started, Marvin Moore rushed out of the station screaming incoherently and waving a pistol. He began pulling the trigger, firing several times. A round smacked me in the chest, right in the middle of my vest as I yanked out my revolver. But the shooting had stopped when I lined up my sights on him. Frosty had rushed up to Moore with his pistol in his hand.

"Drop it," Frosty yelled, "or I'll blow you away."

Moore threw down his gun and ran toward a clearing behind the station. The Kevlar vest that I almost didn't wear had saved my life. I hurt, but I wasn't dead, and I took off after Moore. He bounded over a side ditch, sprinting through brambles toward a pine thicket, where I tackled him face down in the frozen slush and I rode him like a sled. When we stopped, I pulled his hands up behind him and put on the cuffs.

"You're under arrest," I said. "You do not have to make a statement and anything you say may be used against you. You have a right to an attorney, and one will be appointed if you can't afford to hire one. Understand?"

"He understands," Frosty panted. He was standing over us with sweat drops popping out on his forehead. His presence surprised me because I figured he'd go after Dinkins. He was so winded that I feared he might have a heart attack.

"Did you catch Dinkins?" I said.

"No," he said. "Came to help you. Dinkins got away. Last time I saw him he was running through brush over yonder." Frosty pointed toward the station lot.

"You're hurting me," Moore said. "You got the handcuffs too tight and they're cutting my wrists."

"Be still and quit struggling," I said. "You're making them tighter by resisting. Frosty, take this son of a bitch and lock him down in the car. If he gives you any trouble, whack him with your pistol butt. I'm going to see if I can find Dinkins."

Dinkins left a trail of blood that was easy to follow. At first I'd thought he'd injured himself trying to escape. I caught up with him crawling in a briar patch about a hundred yards from his car. His back was soaked with blood and I could see that he was badly hurt.

"Somebody help me." His voice was weak and he wasn't faking. "I'm shot."

I'd left the handset in the car, so I called out to Frosty, hoping he'd be able to hear. "Get an ambulance. Tell them it's ten-thirty-three traffic. Man's been shot."

"Will do," Frosty hollered back and shoved Moore toward the cruiser.

I tried to slow the bleeding with pressure, but that didn't work. The blood kept pouring out.

"Why'd you shoot me?" Dinkins sobbed. "All I did was haul six cases of shine. Hell of a reason to die for." He closed his eyes but he was still breathing.

"If you can hear me," I said, "I wasn't the one who shot you." He showed no indication that he'd heard.

While I waited for an ambulance, I spread my jacket over Dinkins and walked to the cruiser where I got a blanket from the trunk. The sleeping bag would have been warmer, but it was across the highway in the woods. Dinkins was still unconscious when I stretched the blanket over him. His pulse was weak, and he was gasping when the rescue squad showed up. I helped load his body onto a stretcher, knowing that he wouldn't survive. I'd heard my share of death rasps before.

I stepped back to the cruiser and looked inside. Moore was handcuffed in the back seat behind the plastic shield. He bowed his head and hid his face when I shined my flashlight on him. I saw enough to know that he was too small to have been the shooter in the black van.

"I've got his pistol," Frosty said. "He threw it down on the ground. It's a .38 Rossi with a snub nose. He quit shooting because it's empty."

"Did you search him? He might be carrying something else."

"Patted him down. He didn't have nothing else, not even a pocket knife. I wish you'd look at his gun. He's filed off the serial number."

"That's okay," I said. "The lab can lift it with an acid treatment. Bet you ten-to-one it comes back stolen." I was sorry Frosty had put his prints on the weapon.

Riggins arrived a short while later with his blue lights flashing, trailed by a wrecker with blinking yellow lights. The sheriff pulled his Cherokee next to my cruiser and scrutinized the situation from inside, trying to talk through rolled-up windows. When that didn't work, he got out and a gust of frigid air smacked him in the face. He got back inside and motioned for me to join him.

"Heard the radio traffic and called the wrecker. Met the ambulance going to town, but I don't know beans about what happened."

"We've got one man arrested and another on the way to the hospital."

"What the hell—"

"The wounded man, Pete Dinkins, brought a load of whiskey here, and the proprietor of this business shot him. It didn't look like Dinkins is going to make it."

"You didn't shoot—"

"Neither Frosty nor I fired a shot. Marvin Moore, the man handcuffed in the back seat, is the shooter. One of his stray bullets got Dinkins. Another hit my vest. Hell broke loose when Frosty and I drove up on the delivery."

"Did you have a search warrant?" Riggins didn't ask if I'd been injured.

"Didn't need one. Had probable cause that'll stand up in court."

"What kind of probable cause?"

"Information from a reliable source and personal observations."

"You'd better be right," he said.

"Glad you're here. We need help."

"What do you mean?" Riggins raised his eyes and puffed out his lips.

"Either transport Moore to jail or help me inventory the Lincoln.

"I'll help you, since Frosty already has Moore behind the shield."

His answer wasn't a surprise. In my ten years working for him, I'd never seen him make an arrest or handle a prisoner. I got out of the Cherokee and went to the cruiser. Frosty nodded when I asked him to book Moore at the county jail. "Don't let him make bond until we photograph and interview him."

"How're you gonna get back?" Frosty asked.

"Guess I'll ride with Riggins."

"Be careful. Don't say anything he can use against you."

The ignition keys were missing from the Lincoln, and I borrowed a crowbar from the wrecker driver to pop open the trunk, exposing thirty-six gallons of moonshine. Riggins had finally gotten out and walked over to the trunk. He picked up a plastic gallon jug and smiled.

"Try not to handle that," I said. "I'm gonna dust those jugs for prints."

Riggins frowned, but put the jug back.

I found a burlap bag jammed behind the spare tire, and it contained about a pound of homegrown marijuana.

"What are you gonna do with this liquor?" Riggins said. "I ought to keep a little for my own use. It'd be good to give out for Christmas presents to my supporters."

"I'm destroying it, except for a gallon, which we'll use for evidence."

"Don't pour it all out. Looks like it was run through a copper worm. Ought to be good."

"Sheriff, misappropriating evidence can get you in trouble. We need only a gallon for court. Whatever you do, don't even think about keeping any of this for your personal use."

Riggins cupped his hands and blew through them. "I didn't intend to keep any of it." He turned away and went to his Cherokee and called for a ten-twenty-eight on the Lincoln's tag. In a few minutes, he told me the tag came back as having been reported lost or stolen. I looked beneath the windshield for the car's serial number. Someone had filed it off. That meant we'd have to get the state boys to help. They know secret places to find erased numbers.

We didn't leave until midmorning, after I'd dusted the jugs with fingerprint powder. The results were negative but I'd found that damp plastic rarely yields prints on cold mornings.

Using my pocket knife, I ripped a piece of carpet from the trunk to compare with the fibers taken from Joe's clothing. Gloria radioed that Dinkins was DOA at the hospital. Moore now faced murder charges. The bad thing was that Dinkins died probably thinking I'd killed him.

"Two murders in a little over a week," Riggins said mostly to himself as he pulled into the courthouse parking lot. "It doesn't look good with an election next year. They might say that I'm not doing my job."

"You've got one solved," I said. "Marvin Moore rushed out shooting, and it was his bullet that killed Dinkins. We'll get the lab to confirm this."

"Will it be from the same gun that killed Joe Sacks?"

"The lab might be able to tell us."

"Good," said Riggins. "That's something I can tell the media."

"Before you call the press, ask Gloria to run a records check on Moore. She can get his birth date from Frosty. He's got Moore's billfold. Then call Hokie and get him to prepare a warrant for murder. He can add attempted murder to it. The bastard tried to kill me and would have but for the vest."

"Aren't you gonna wait for the lab report?"

"No. I saw and heard him shoot the pistol. What's more, he was the only one who fired a shot."

"I'll run this by Hokie. Don't want to make a mistake with elections next year."

"Another thing. Let's notify Dinkins's next of kin, if we can find any. He has a brother, Mike, but I'm not sure where to locate him."

CHAPTER
Sixteen

Moore sat hunkered down on his bunk when the jailer unlocked the door for Frosty and me to enter his cell. He looked up when the door swung open. Before I could Mirandize him again, he glared at me through murky, spaced-out eyes. "I ain't talking to nobody until I get a lawyer. You're all out to get me." He had stubby dark whiskers that hadn't bearded out.

"Have it your way," I said. "Dinkins didn't make it and you're facing the biggie, murder one."

"When do I get to make my phone call? I know my rights. I want a lawyer now."

"Soon as we leave, you can make a call," I said. "And you'd better get a good lawyer, because you'll need a magician. Your hearing will likely be this afternoon."

"Not without a lawyer," he said. "And I'll hire my own attorney."

"Hard head makes a soft ass," Frosty muttered as we left.

Riggins was standing by the window in his private office, looking at the barren terraced garden on the backside of the courthouse. He turned slowly when Frosty and I walked through his open door. There was a blank look on his face, and it took him a second or so to focus on us.

"Hokie wants you to brief him soon as you can so he can prepare a murder warrant," Riggins said. He took a deep breath and exhaled. "And Gloria got a hit on Moore with the computer."

"Then he does have a track record?" I said.

"Been convicted of assault with a deadly weapon and attempted murder in North Carolina, and has spent eight of his twenty-nine years behind bars."

"I could tell he wasn't no Sunday school teacher," Frosty said. "He refused to sign his fingerprint cards."

"He's wild," I said, "or he wouldn't have come out shooting. Just crazy as hell."

"I'm glad he's from North Carolina," Riggins said. "He won't have family to vote against me."

"We'd better notify Dinkins's next of kin before the media gets to them," I said.

"Gloria's working on it." The worry wrinkles plowed through Riggins's brow. "Do you think I'm going to get sued over this? Hokie says we're in the clear, but he might be wrong. Hope that you and Frosty don't have me in deep shit."

I shrugged and went out to my desk, pulled out a chair, slid into it, and scribbled down notes before leaving for Hokie's office. It suited me that he was personally preparing the affidavits to draw the warrant. As a lawyer, he'd be better at putting in all the legal mumbo jumbo and Latin words that the courts like. Frosty stayed so that he could store the evidence.

"I called the judge and got us a hearing set for this afternoon," Hokie said when I got there. "Guess who she's appointed to represent Moore?"

"Got no idea," I said. "But we don't have more than a dozen lawyers in the county."

"The honorable J. R. Taylor will be his counsel."

"Moore talked like he wanted to hire his own counselor," I said.

"No, he decided to let the taxpayers foot the bill."

"At least he's got somebody who'll yell and cry for him." Taylor had been my nemesis for years, ever since I busted the Dinkins brothers for jacklighting deer.

"J.R. tries to tear down the credibility of his opposition," Hokie said. "Uses the old scattergun approach."

Hokie took a ballpoint pen and wrote as I supplied him with facts about the shooting. In about forty-five minutes when he finished, we walked across the courthouse square to a portable trailer that housed the magistrate's office. I placed my left hand on a Bible, raised my right hand, and swore the facts in the affidavit were true and correct to the best of my knowledge. The magistrate issued the warrants, and we headed for the courtroom.

J.R. Taylor was leaning over in his chair and whispering to Moore at the defense table. He extended me a square-jawed glare when I sat next to Hokie. I patted myself on the back for not giving him my middle finger. He was wearing a tan sports coat and a red bow tie that I thought was too young for a man of fifty.

"We want this hearing continued," he stood and told Judge Rebecca Tillinhast.

Her face flushed. "Continuance is a crutch for a weak defense, or means that the defendant hadn't paid his lawyer. Neither should apply here since the county is paying you and this is only a preliminary hearing to determine probable cause."

"Your Honor, I need time to confer with my client."

I figured Taylor wanted to milk the system with interview time—about a hundred bucks an hour.

"If you postpone it too long," Hokie said, "we won't need a hearing. I'll get a grand-jury indictment."

"We know the rules." Taylor rubbed his hands over his potbelly and fingered a gold watch chain. "I also request that you set a reasonable bond for my client."

"The commonwealth objects to any bond," Hokie fired back.

Taylor raised his hands. "My client has a business to operate."

"Yes," Hokie said, "an illegal liquor business."

"I object to Mr. Preston's comment. My client isn't charged with running an illegal liquor business."

"We can add that if you want," Hokie said. "We didn't include it because we didn't want to clutter up the docket."

Taylor tried a different approach. "My client isn't going to run away. He says he'll be in court anytime you say."

"This is a murder charge," Hokie said. "We request the defendant be denied bond." By then Hokie had risen from his chair, something he doesn't always do in district court. "The man is a convicted felon from North Carolina. If his feet hit the ground, he'll fly away faster than a Canada goose. In addition to our murder warrant, federal firearm charges may be pending. I'm sure the U.S. Attorney's office will file a detainer."

Taylor looked surprised. "He didn't tell me he had a record."

"May I approach the bench?" Hokie said.

When the judge nodded, he marched forward with Moore's rap sheet, and Taylor followed with a bewildered look on his face.

"Are you sure we're talking about the same man?" Taylor said.

"Not only does he have a record," Hokie said, "but he hasn't cooperated in the least with the arresting officers. He refused to sign his fingerprint cards."

Judge Tillinhast, a wrinkled-faced woman in her mid-fifties, ordered Moore to stand up. "As your attorney knows," she began, "this will be a hearing to decide probable cause. All I have to do is to determine that a crime was committed and you could be the culprit. I do not try felony cases. The commonwealth attorney does not have to prove you guilty beyond a reasonable doubt in my court. He only has to show probable cause. If a grand jury indicts you, a higher court will pass judgment."

"I've explained that to my client," Taylor said.

"Tell me when you'll be ready for me to hear this matter. Or do you want to waive?" Her impatience showed. "I'm ordering your client held without bond until we have a hearing. Make up your mind when you want a date set."

"How about tomorrow?" Taylor said. "That'll allow me time to confer with Mr. Moore."

"Unless the commonwealth objects," the judge said, "I'm setting the hearing for nine in the morning."

After we left, Hokie said he wanted ballistics reports on the firearm and the bullet as soon as possible. "Just want to show the court beyond any doubt that his gun fired the fatal shot. It wouldn't hurt if we did ballistics on yours and Frosty's guns."

"You don't think Frosty or I shot Dinkins?" I said.

"No, but surprises burst forth at trials, and it's best to cover everything. What if Taylor says his client didn't shoot Dinkins? He can't argue with ballistics."

"I'll call Doc Lee and see if he's dug out the bullet yet. Need to go by the hospital anyhow. My chest hurts where that bullet hit my vest."

Hokie nodded. "You can make one trip do for two."

"If Doc's got it, we'll hand-deliver it with the firearm to the state lab, and they may be able to lift the serial number on the gun at the same time."

Doc was relaxing in his office chair when I got there. He still was wearing his working clothes, a green scrub suit, and smiled when he saw me. On his desk, he pointed to the slug he'd taken from Dinkins's upper back. "It won't be from the same gun that killed Sacks. Looks like this came from an old barrel with worn grooves and lands. That's unofficial, of course."

I left his office and went to the ER and let them check out the bruises on my chest. A young Oriental doc with a bright smile told me I'd be okay in a few days and not to worry. But I did worry as I left the hospital. Someone would have to take the bullet and pistol to the lab at Richmond, a six-hour drive. Frosty would be the logical one to go since he made the seizure and locked it in our evidence room. This would simplify the chain of custody. I knew Frosty hated trips and wouldn't go if he could avoid it.

Riggins was looking at a *Progressive Farmer* magazine when I got back to the office. He pitched the magazine on the desk and cranked his head in my direction. "Did Hokie say we had a good case?"

"Yes, but he wants us to take the murder weapon to the lab in Richmond. Doc Lee has a slug to go with it. It would help the chain of custody if Frosty took it."

"Frosty can't go," Riggins said. "He's too far behind on serving all these civil papers. You can't go either."

"Hokie wants ballistics tests done right away."

"Don't worry. I'll go myself. The legislature is still in session. It'd look better if I went, me being the high sheriff. Did Moore waive his hearing?"

"No. The judge set it for nine in the morning."

"Can you handle it without me?"

"Sure, won't be difficult showing probable cause on this one. Frosty and I were eyewitnesses."

"Then you don't need me. Since you and Frosty are busy, I'll leave Billy Bob Perkins in charge until I get back." Riggins dismissed me with a wave of his hand and picked up his phone to call Billy Bob.

"We should get a search warrant for the Orange Fix-It Shop."

"No," he said. "Unless Hokie orders it, I don't want us more involved. You can check it out with Billy Bob."

"He's never investigated a murder."

"Like it or not, he's your boss until I get back."

I didn't reply. He was the sheriff's nephew. The only good thing about this was that he rarely came to town.

CHAPTER
Seventeen

The sheriff had ruined my appetite, and I drove past Maggie's without stopping for supper. To my knowledge, Billy Bob had investigated one case, and that involved the theft of a coon dog. I went straight home and decided to pour myself two fingers of bourbon over some ice. The red light on the answering machine was blinking, but I needed a drink before checking it out.

The first call came from Hokie, and he wanted to talk right away. A second message was a twangy male voice delivering a death threat. He clicked off and didn't bother to leave a name or say why I was going to die. He'd called, I assumed, from a public booth, or my call identifier would have registered the number. I dialed Hokie's house.

"Got something you need to know," he said. "J.R. Taylor stopped by my office this afternoon complaining that you were going to kill his client. Moore says you were the reason he came out shooting. Taylor claims you've made open threats."

For a second I couldn't answer. I held the phone in my hand and pondered. "It's a lie," I finally said. "I haven't threatened to kill Moore or anybody else."

"Not saying you did. I'm only repeating Taylor's accusations. He wants you investigated by the attorney general's office."

"The attorney general's office?"

"He's already made a phone call to the AG."

"You've got my report," I told him. "Except for the informant's identity, all the facts are there."

"I read it. Even showed it to Taylor because he'd get to see it anyhow under the rules of discovery. He wants you suspended until the state investigates his charges."

"Give me a polygraph test."

"No. I'm not buckling under to Taylor or any other defense lawyer. He's put the integrity of the system at stake. By submitting you to a polygraph, I'd show that I didn't have faith in your word."

"If he makes enough noise, Riggins won't support me."

"Probably not. That's why I'm glad Taylor asked the attorney general to investigate. At least you should get a fair shake."

"Do I need a lawyer?"

"You're on the county payroll. I'm your lawyer."

"Riggins is leaving early in the morning for Richmond," I said. "Taking Moore's pistol and the slug to the lab."

"Well, he can't suspend you if he's out of town."

"Moore is lying. Didn't even know his name until a few days before the raid."

"Taylor might be mouthy, but he didn't put his client up to making these charges."

"Maybe he didn't," I said, "but somebody's lying, and by the way, I got a threatening message on my answering machine. Said I was a dead man."

"Without a badge, you might be. Everybody knows you. Did you see Beth Sawyer's news tonight?"

"No, I didn't get home until just now."

"Your face was plastered across the screen."

"I didn't talk to any reporters. Seen them do a number on too many people. Where'd they get my picture?"

"Probably used file film. No doubt they'll be at the hearing."

After we hung up, I tried to figure why Moore concocted that story since I'd never had any previous contact with him. I'd check him out good before the sheriff suspended me, even if I had to go all the way to North Carolina.

The phone rang and I grabbed the receiver. "Hello."

"You made the news." Tina's voice sounded soft.

"Are you back in town?"

"No," she said. "I'm at my apartment."

"Thought you had a lot of Christmas parties set up."

"I did until I saw you on the six o'clock news. You lead an exciting life."

"Wish I was at a Christmas party instead of being in the middle of this mess."

"Mine weren't much fun. Does this latest case involve the same people who threatened me?"

"I don't know," I said. "Nothing is making sense."

"If I come tomorrow, will you take me back to Horse Heaven?"

"Don't come tomorrow. At nine, I've got a preliminary hearing. Then I'll be tied up putting together a homicide case. Looks like everything's breaking at once."

She said she'd get back in touch by the end of the week. I didn't tell her Riggins may have taken my badge by then. The thought of it gnawed my guts into knots, but I was too old to cry.

"Before I hang up," she said, "there weren't any signs of spent mash in the water samples from Horse Heaven."

"So much for speculation," I said.

Her call was businesslike, but it made me feel better. I was thinking of Tina when I hit the sack at midnight. Sleep came quickly, but it didn't last very long. A noise I couldn't identify woke me. Raising my head, I listened and heard the drone of an idling motor in my driveway. And without turning on a light, I got up and tiptoed to a front window. I slid back a curtain and cranked it open. All I saw was the night's blackness, but I heard the motor. After I picked up my shotgun, I opened the window wider and heard a man say, "Let's get out of here. I think I heard a noise at his trailer." Then I heard a door slam.

I watched as the taillights of a pickup truck departed, kicking up my gravel. Then I went outside for a quick look. I didn't use a light in case they'd left somebody behind to snipe me. And I listened a long time before going back inside and propping the shotgun next to my bed. I'd look more thoroughly when it was daylight.

Before I dozed, I called Frosty and warned him in case he'd been included on the hit list. "I've had visitors outside my window, but they're gone now. Don't know what they did, but I'll find out in the morning."

"Probably it was a couple of lovebirds," Frosty said.

"They might pay you a visit. Also, somebody left me a death threat on my answering machine."

"That's why I don't have an answering machine. I don't want death threats."

"It's not a joke."

"With my night light, nobody could do much sneaking up on me. Besides, my dogs bark at everything. Want me to drive over and bring you a guard dog? Sounds like you need a baby-sitter."

"Thanks, but no," I replied. "I'm staying put until daylight. I'd hate to stumble across a trip wire if they planted a bomb."

"This ain't Vietnam. I'll come by first thing in the morning before the hearing."

CHAPTER
Eighteen

The next morning, I saw where the visitors had punched holes in all four tires on my cruiser. I looked carefully and figured that they'd used an ice pick. The hood was still locked in place, and I couldn't see any signs that they'd broken into the cruiser.

Next, I went to a shed behind my trailer and checked my '82 Ford pickup truck. Its bright red paint didn't have as much as a scratch. That truck was my pride and joy, and I'd named her the Red Bullet.

Much to my belly's delight, Frosty arrived bringing two country-ham biscuits and coffee from Maggie's. As I ate the food, he retraced my steps, saying he wanted to be sure that I hadn't overlooked more damage. "You're lucky that was all they done."

"Yeah," I said. "I must've spooked them when I opened a window."

Frosty got on his radio and took care of having new tires brought out. I rode with him to the courthouse for the hearing. Riggins, he said, had stopped at Maggie's earlier and now was on his way to Richmond. "I didn't say nothing to him about somebody being at your place last night," he said.

A television news truck occupied the sheriff's spot at the courthouse parking lot, and people were bunched together around the entrance. I presumed that the cluster of people were there for the murder hearing. Nothing this big had happened in my ten years with the sheriff's department. To reach the courtroom, I had to shoulder my way through a bottleneck of spectators saturating the hallway. A television cameraman, wrestling with his lighting equipment, almost tripped me with wiring he'd spread across the floor. A young woman pushed a mike in front of me. "Deputy Stark, will you talk on camera for us?"

"No comment," I said, moving past her without looking back. She followed me into the courtroom, where the pewlike benches already were overflowing like a Sunday night revival.

"I'm Beth Sawyer," she said. "Are they moving the hearing to the Circuit Court facilities? There's not room for everybody here."

I shrugged, looked at the high ceiling, and kept moving.

"Will you talk to me after the hearing?" she said.

I didn't reply.

By taking a shortcut, Frosty had beat me to the courtroom. He was sitting beside Hokie at the prosecution table. Moore sat with Taylor at another table across the aisle. Taylor, with his bald head shining, drummed his fingers on a stack of law books piled in front of him. He shot me a glare, a reminder of his contempt. Spectators were nosily muttering as the courtroom awaited the arrival of the judge.

In a deep but loud voice, the bailiff called for everyone to rise. "Oh yes, oh yes, oh yes," he sang, "this honorable court is now in session with the Honorable Judge Rebecca Tillinhast presiding. . . ." She made her entry through a rear door, swirling her dark robe, and climbed the steps to the bench. She rapped with her gavel and everything got quiet.

"The judge is not letting the cameras inside," Hokie whispered to me. "Go out the side door if you want to avoid them."

Before I could pull up a chair, Taylor arose. "Your Honor," he began, "I have discussed the case against Mr. Moore with the commonwealth attorney. At this time, I'd like to waive a preliminary hearing."

A hush prevailed in the room. "Very well," Judge Tillinhast said. "I'm binding this case over to the grand jury."

"Will you consider setting bond for my client?"

"Again, I object," Hokie said. "The man is charged with first-degree murder."

Judge Tillinhast looked over her half-sized glasses and frowned. "Mr. Taylor," she said, "I'm ordering your client held without bond. If you don't like my decision, you can appeal to the Circuit Court."

"I'm sure I will appeal," Taylor said with a scowl.

Hokie winked at me. "He won't appeal. That's just bluster."

"There's more to this case that will be investigated," Taylor said.

Judge Tillinhast raised and lowered her gavel. "That will be all, Mr. Taylor."

Hokie stood, smiled, and thanked the judge for her ruling.

I watched the jailer lead Moore away through the same side door Frosty had used to beat me inside the courtroom. To avoid the crowd, I followed, leaving Hokie to face the media. With Riggins gone, he could have the spotlight.

I stopped at the coffee machine, got a cup of joe, and then started upstairs. I heard heels clicking behind me so I moved faster. I didn't look, but I figured it was Beth Sawyer.

"What's up?" I said to Gloria at the office.

"You've had a long-distance phone call."

"From Blacksburg?"

"Not this time," she said. "I wrote down the number for you. You may want to use the sheriff's private phone. I think it was from your ex-wife."

"Must be something bad because I don't hear from her otherwise," I said.

"Maybe you forgot to send your child support."

"Never been late on that."

My stomach twitched as I called Mildred. It rang a half dozen times before she picked up. "We need three thousand dollars," she told me. "Frank Jr. has an appointment with an orthodontist."

"An orthodontist? He's nineteen years old. Braces are for little kids." Three thousand dollars would use up my savings. If Riggins suspended me, I'd need that money for survival.

"George is willing to pay," she said. "But Frank is your son. I thought paying for the braces ought to be up to you." George, her third husband, was okay, but I didn't want him to usurp my role as father.

"Why does he need braces at this age?" I said. "I thought I paid for braces when he was ten."

"You did. Now Frank wants to become an actor. To make it as a leading man, he needs perfect teeth."

"An actor? The last time he and I discussed careers he wanted to be a fireman."

"For Pete's sake, he was thirteen years old then. Now he has a chance to get a scholarship at DePaul."

"Thought he was going to Appalachian State on a basketball scholarship?"

"That was before he got a leading part in a Little Theater play."

I remembered when I acted in high school plays. It had never crossed my mind to be a professional, so I'd joined the army. "It'll flatten my wallet, but I'll send the money." Ernest Borgnine made it big in acting, I thought, and he sure as hell didn't have perfect teeth.

When I came out of Riggins's office, Paul Simmons was waiting at my desk. He handed me a lined notepad sheet on which somebody had scribbled a letter to the editor about me. I couldn't tell if it'd been written by an illiterate person, or by somebody pretending to be illiterate. In either case, it accused me of planning to kill Marvin Moore.

"This letter is a lie. Are you printing it?"

"No. My paper doesn't publish unsigned letters. I'm showing it to you for your information. You've really pissed off somebody. Who's after you?"

"Don't know. Off the record, I received a threat on my answering machine. All this started after I began investigating Joe Sacks's murder."

"I'm not printing this letter because it wasn't signed."
He took the letter back and stuffed it in his shirt pocket.
"Understand that I'm not shielding you from any
legitimate accusations."

After Simmons left, Gloria said, "Was your long-
distance call bad news?"

"Nowadays, all my calls bring bad news. Frank Junior
wants to become an actor and needs three thousand dollars
to fix his teeth. I'll have to rob my credit union account."

"You have that much in savings?"

"Yeah," I said, "but it'll leave me broke."

She shrugged. "Thank goodness I never had children.
But I've got that old Chevy, and it's almost as expensive as
children."

I changed the subject. "According to Moore's rap sheet,
his last conviction was for attempted murder in Chatham
County, North Carolina. I'm heading there this afternoon
while I've still got a badge."

"Better clear it with Billy Bob before you leave," Gloria
said. "Riggins did leave him in charge."

"No," I said. "Billy Bob wouldn't have the guts to okay
the trip."

"Don't say I didn't warn you."

"You can do me a favor. Call Chatham County and find
out if the sheriff's department remembers Moore."

While she made the call, I reviewed Moore's personal
history sheet. Frosty had recorded that Clarkie Sue Brown
of Bonlee was next of kin. He listed her as Moore's
grandmother. That could be a starting point, I thought.

Gloria returned the receiver to its cradle. "Deputy
Kenneth Oxindine worked the case against Moore. He'll be
on patrol, and they'll call him to meet you at the Siler City
police department when you get there."

"I'll contact you when I check in," I said.

"You're pushing your luck. The boss won't like you
spending county money without his okay."

"Gonna pay for the room myself."

"You're taking the county car and wearing the county uniform."

"You're right," I said as I walked out.

I found Frosty talking to the county administrator's secretary and got him to drive me to my repaired cruiser at home. I didn't tell him that I was leaving town, so he could truthfully tell Riggins he didn't know about my trip.

In less than an hour I had filled up at the county gas pumps and was driving south toward North Carolina.

CHAPTER
Nineteen

A scattering of skinny pine trees and fenced pastures greeted me four hours later when I arrived in Chatham County. The sky was furrowed with pinkish clouds reflecting the gentle red clay hills below. Frosty said that a pink sky at night was a sailor's delight. If so, no inclement weather was in sight.

I stopped at a phone booth. The sheriff's dispatcher said Deputy Oxindine would be waiting at the Siler City PD, and he was. He was standing next to his cruiser and waved his hand when I pulled up and parked. Oxindine had straight black hair and elevated cheekbones. His deep-set black eyes reached into my soul when he walked over to shake hands. I guessed him to be under thirty.

"In case you're wondering, I'm a Lumbee Indian—not Hispanic." His angular body moved with the lively step of a shortstop.

I nodded. "Knew some Lumbees when I was with the Charlotte Police Department a few years back. Never saw one who couldn't swing his fists."

"My ancestor was Henry Berry Lowery, a warrior chief who'd make the Outlaw Josey Wales look tame."

I went straight to my reason for being there. "Do you remember arresting Marvin Moore for attempted murder?"

"Sure. He shot a Mexican his grandmother had hired to cut Christmas trees."

"What was the deal on that?"

"Marvin convinced himself that Mexicans were aliens from outer space, plotting to get him. He's a real fruitcake."

"We've charged him with murder. He listed his grandmother, Clarkie Sue Brown of Bonlee, as next of kin. How far is Bonlee?"

"About eight miles down the road. We can use my cruiser because I'm on duty until midnight. Clarkie Sue lives alone in an old abandoned school building she bought at public auction. She added a front porch and lowered the ceilings . . . cheaper to heat."

"Let me check in at the Holiday Inn, and give my office my ten-twenty. Then I'll be ready to go."

"Be waiting in the parking lot."

After I'd registered and dropped off my suitcase, I telephoned Gloria at her residence since it was after four and she'd gone home. I gave her my whereabouts, and she said she hadn't mentioned my trip to anyone, not even Frosty.

To reach Bonlee we took a blacktop road lined with poplar trees and paralleling a railroad track.

"The Atlantic Coast Line built that track to freight rabbits out of Chatham County," Oxindine said. "But the rabbits are gone now—damned chemicals and fescue grasses have wiped them out. Man couldn't make a living trapping them anymore."

He pulled up to an old wooden building sitting on the outskirts of Bonlee. "This is Clarkie Sue Brown's house," he said.

After he checked out of service, we got out of his cruiser and ascended a flight of concrete block steps, and were on her front porch. He gently rapped twice on the door, and she called for us to enter. She was sitting in a rocking chair in the middle of a big room, next to the entry hall. She was a small, wrinkled woman lit up by a swag lamp that hung from the ceiling on a corded chain. Her long white hair was pulled back and tied into a granny knot. With a bonnet she could have doubled for my own grandmother.

"Excuse my manners," she said. "I'm piecing together a quilt, and I've got this material spread so I can reach it. If I got up, it'd take thirty minutes to rearrange it when I sat back down." She was surrounded by paper grocery bags, each stuffed with tiny scraps of cloth. Plowed folds across her forehead and a short, thin nose framed her drooping eyes. Hers was a face that had seen its share of misery.

"My name is Frank Stark." I handed her a card with my name and phone number.

"I'm Clarkie Sue Brown," she said, "and I know Mr. Oxindine. His grandfather used to help me with my Christmas trees. Of course, I don't have that many now."

"Mrs. Brown," I said.

"It's Miss Brown, but better yet, call me Clarkie Sue. Everyone else does."

"I'm here about Marvin Moore, your grandson. He's facing a murder charge up in Virginia."

"Oh my goodness," she said. "He's always been a troubled boy, and I'm so sorry that he's killed someone."

"What can you tell me about his background?"

"I had to ask him to move out. Marvin wouldn't take his pills, and he acted crazy when he didn't. That medicine the state doctor gave him made him as normal as you'd want anybody to be. Without those pills, he thought everybody was spying on him."

"He was convicted of attempted murder," I said.

"They shoulda put him in Dix Hill, our state mental hospital over in Raleigh. He was always hearing voices talking to him. Thought the voices were coming from outer space. I'd hired a Mexican to trim the tops from my pine trees. Marvin thought he was planting listening devices and shot him in the back with a shotgun. Thank the Lord the poor man recovered."

Seeing her eyes water, I knew that these memories were painful, an anguish that quilting needles couldn't mend. Her bony fingers continued to sew together the various colored patches as she talked. "I blame myself for him being like he is," she said. "His mother, Dorothy, was born to me out of wedlock. Back in those days, people didn't accept that as good behavior. My mother and father were respectable, and they didn't accept it, either. But they did will me this land since I was their only child.

"Dorothy thought people around here looked down on her. And I guess they did. When she was sixteen, she ran off with a GI from Fort Bragg. They got married about a month before Marvin was born. She left him here and just walked out the door, and I haven't heard from her since.

"It was tough raising him on my small income. Besides selling trees, I make a little from these quilts. Neighbors give me their scraps of cloth. Got just enough in a savings account to keep me off food stamps and to get me buried."

For a little while she quit talking and stared at a smelly unvented oil heater with a water pan on top. She said, "The saddest thing is that I've got forty acres of land here to leave to somebody. It's not much, but they aren't making any more land. It could have been Marvin's."

"Did he ever hold down a job?"

"Not for long," she said. "He flipped hamburgers at Hardee's when he was younger. Then he got a job fixing cars at Crawford's Garage until he had a falling out with the Crawfords. He worked awhile around a sawmill, fixing their equipment when it broke down. I tried to get him to go to school, but he wouldn't. Quit in the sixth grade."

"Why did he move to Virginia?" I said. "Do you have relatives there?"

"He made some friends, I guess, working at that sawmill," she said. "He doesn't have any kin but me, at least that I know about."

"Did you meet his friends or learn any of their names?"

"Nope," she said. "I didn't want him hanging around if he didn't take his medicine. My nerves couldn't take him being suspicious of everybody."

"Where'd he get the money to open a filling station?"

"He might not read good," she said, "but he can count money. He saved most of what he made. I think he got good pay at the sawmill. He wasn't lazy and he can fix anything."

"Do you have any of his prescription left?" I said.

She nodded toward to a wall cabinet. "Over there."

Oxindine and I looked in the cabinet and saw a small bottle behind a jar of Tums. I examined it. The state prison pharmacy had labeled it with instructions for Moore to take one every morning. I guessed there must have been a hundred pills left in the bottle. It didn't appear that he'd taken many of them.

"It says Haldol on the bottle," Oxindine said.

"Yes," she said. "That's it."

I pulled out a notepad and scratched down the data from the bottle—the name of the pharmacist, date of the prescription and its number. I also wrote the name of the prison's psychiatrist. Oxindine said the doctor had a Siler City office and worked for the state part-time under contract.

"You can take the bottle," she said. "It doesn't sound like my grandson is coming back soon. Even if he did, he wouldn't take that medicine."

"You keep it," I said. "It wouldn't be legal for me to have it in my possession without a court order."

I thanked Oxindine for his help when we returned to Siler City. I left him to do his patrol and went straight to my room to change into civvies. I was thirsty for a cold beer.

To get to the lounge, I passed a banquet room reserved for a private Christmas party. Inside, I heard a combination of laughter and music, causing me to think of Tina.

Surprisingly, the bar wasn't crowded. I figured the in-crowd was celebrating privately. There were a dozen or so people scattered about the horseshoe bar in the dimly lit room, made hazy by cigarette smoke. Their voices overpowered a piped-in Tennessee Ernie Ford recording of "Silent Night." I sat on a stool next to a talkative local who complained that soon everybody in Siler City would be speaking Spanish. I didn't comment but let him buy me a second beer while he jabbered. It was my fee for being a good listener. He'd mistaken me for a truck driver who'd parked a big rig out front, and wanted me to know that his brother drove for Consolidated Freight. I shrugged when he asked if my mirrors were long enough to reach when I was pulling doubles. His brother hated doubles, he said, because the dock people never loaded them correctly.

The beer was very cold, the way I liked it. It dulled my senses better than a tranquilizer. Believe it or not, I found his constant drone relaxing. He said that he was recently divorced and down in the dumps. I'd been there and done that. All I had to do was sip beer and respond with an occasional grunt or nod. In a little while, I knew everything he knew. I was glad he didn't notice my lodge ring in case he, too, was a brother. That would have involved more conversation than I wanted.

I jumped into the shower when I got back to my room, and I let the hot water run down my body for ten minutes. It felt good because I didn't have to worry about draining my well. Tomorrow, I'd contact Dr. Ray Shackleford. I was mellow, and sleep came quickly.

The next morning, after looking up the doctor's office address, I stopped at a long table set up in the lobby for what the inn called a continental breakfast. The clerk said it went with the room, but I expected more than orange juice, coffee, and a slice of fruit. Oh yeah, they had some muffins and sweet rolls. But at least I didn't have to pay extra for it.

The doctor's name was displayed on a white sign with black lettering. His office was in a row of several medical facilities inserted in a relatively new brick building. An adjoining parking lot was full, so I left my cruiser at a Shell station across the street. The door to his office was locked. I pushed a plastic button that made a bell ring inside.

Dr. Shackleford unbolted the door. He was tall and skinny with long blond hair that was beginning to gray. My uniform caused him to do a double take. "Anything the matter?"

"If I could," I said, "I'd like to talk to you about a former patient." I gave him one of my cards.

"At first, I thought you were from the local prison camp. Uniforms look the same to me. I'm off until after

Christmas, but you never know what'll come up. I'm kind of busy doing my charts."

"Don't mean to impose, but I need to know about Marvin Moore."

"What do you want to know? I recommended him for parole."

"Anything you can tell me. Up in Ottway County, Virginia, we've got him charged with first-degree murder."

"By law, my sessions with patients are confidential, even inmates in the penal system. I'm afraid I can't help you."

"I need documentation showing that he's—well—er—not always functional."

"You meant to say nuts." Dr. Shackleford smiled. "He wasn't nuts while on medication."

"He killed a man," I said, "and I don't know if he was or wasn't on medication. I need to document his mental condition."

"If I were you, I'd go to the courthouse and get a transcript. Both the prosecution and defense had psychiatrists testifying to find out if he were competent to stand trial. In treating him, I reviewed their reports. All of it is public record."

When we parted, I thought about the three thousand dollars for Frank Jr.'s teeth. I might need part of that money to pay for transcripts if Hokie didn't order them. I realized that I may have overextended myself when I told Gloria I'd pay my own way. Trial transcripts aren't free.

I used the pay phone at the Shell station and made a credit-card call to Gloria. If anything had happened, I wanted to know then. I don't like surprises, not the bad kind anyway.

"Tina Jordan will be in town for the rest of the week," Gloria said. "Nothing else. Frosty asked where you were, and I told him out of town on business."

"Heard from Riggins?"

"He's already called this morning. Says he has to stay over in Richmond until tomorrow."

"Did he say anything about the ballistics report?"

"Yes. He said the lab is certain Moore's pistol and the slug taken from Dinkins match."

"How about the bullet that killed Joe Sacks?"

"They don't think so. That's why he said he was staying over. They want to run another test on that one."

He was staying that extra day to visit his married daughter living there, I figured.

CHAPTER
Twenty

I pushed the accelerator just enough to make the wheels turn at fifty-five as I drove home. I wasn't up to badging my way out of a speeding ticket, and I sure as hell didn't have the money to pay one off. At two o'clock, I passed into Burnsville's greater town limits, and drove straight to Hokie's office across from the courthouse.

His door was standing open, so I walked in. And there sat Hokie, leaning back in a swivel chair holding a glass of liquor. His nose glowed as he gave me a lopsided smile while his glassy eyes peered obliquely. I saw that he was tooted.

"Don't mind if I have a snort, do you?" he said. His brown camel sports coat was rumpled, and he'd spilled whiskey on the front of his shirt. "My secretary is off today, and my wife is running that damned vacuum cleaner at home. Can't stand the noise, so here I am. You're lucky to catch me." He tilted up the glass and took a deep swig. Some spilled and yellowed his silver mustache. Then he poured a chaser of tap water from a pitcher, and turned the glass up. "An old lady once told me she knew her son didn't drink because he liked ice water early in the mornings."

"You must like ice water," I said.

"Won't know until tomorrow morning. And I won't know for sure until I get my phone bill. Usually, I call everybody who survived the war with me. I went to law school, and for a long time I didn't think about any of them. Now that I'm getting old, I remember the old Rainbow Division better."

After he settled down, I told him about my trip and what I'd learned. "I think we need transcripts from

Moore's trial to show that he's paranoid. The psychiatrist wouldn't talk because of his patient's confidentiality."

"I'll subpoena him," Hokie said. "Of course, we might not need the transcripts nor the psychiatrist. With the information you've given me, I can probably break Moore on cross-examination."

I wondered if he could subpoena across state lines, but I didn't bring it up because I wasn't sure Hokie wanted to think that intensely right then. "How are you going to cross-examine him if he doesn't take the witness stand?"

"If he doesn't testify," Hokie said, "there aren't any charges against you. J.R. Taylor can't testify himself and still be the attorney of record. Believe me, that's one lawyer who won't lose a client, not when the county's paying him."

"If you don't need the transcripts, I probably went to Chatham County for nothing."

"Not at all. With what you've found out, I can tear Moore apart if he testifies. You did good."

I wasn't convinced that Hokie understood me, so I excused myself and went to the sheriff's office. Gloria had told me Tina was in town and I thought I'd give her a buzz. Before I picked up the phone, Beth Sawyer, the Channel Three reporter, dashed into the office with hungry, owlish eyes and sat in a chair across from me.

"Did you know J.R. Taylor said you threatened to kill his client?" Her demeanor was deceiving, but below the girlish charisma I saw a shark who'd rip me apart for a news scoop. For a few moments I regarded her features, a pug nose and blond hair that was dark around the roots. Her lipstick was too red, and she wore too much eye shadow.

"Don't have any statement to make," I said, not supplying her with fuel to continue the conversation. "Go interview somebody else."

"Talk off the record." She bared gleaming white teeth, and I thought maybe Frank Jr. could be a newscaster if he flunked out of acting school. She curved her lean body around in the chair and showed me some nice legs. "We could be a team."

"Sorry, but I work alone."

I got up and slipped into Riggins's office, closing the door behind me. I picked up the phone. Might as well call Tina, I told myself. She couldn't do more than shoot me down in flames, and I already had a cauliflower heart. The receptionist at the health department put me through to her extension.

"It's Frank," I said. "Just got back in town."

"Left you a message. I was surprised you weren't around."

"You're not going back out there, are you?"

"We need to meet and talk about that," she said.

"Want me to come over?"

"No, I've got reports to finish and you'd be a distraction. I checked into the Riverview Inn, and I'll be here for the rest of the week."

"Then let's have supper tonight at my place. It's private and I'll serve you either a steak or roast a chicken, Greek style."

"You can cook Greek chicken?"

"Sure. I even use real garlic and olive oil."

"Do you serve baklava as an after-dinner delight?"

"Hey, I'm a cookbook Greek, not a native. But I do make a decent Greek salad."

"Your offer sounds wonderful. Won't your neighbors gossip?"

"Nearest neighbor is half a mile away. You'd really have to be looking to find my place. My trailer sits in the middle of five acres the bank and I jointly own, except I pay the taxes." I didn't mention that I could pee off my front steps without being seen by passing traffic.

"How do I get there?"

"In my car," I said. "I'll be by at seven."

On the way home, I picked up a bottle of Merlot and a canister of oregano. You can't cook like a Greek without oregano. I wasn't sure red wine should be served with poultry, but doctors say it's good for the heart.

Before I opened my door, I made sure there had been no more uninvited guests prowling around. After I looked, I turned the key in the dead-bolt lock, swung open the door, and went inside. The answering machine light was blinking, and I found two calls waiting. My ex had called a couple of hours earlier, and Good Time had left a message saying that he'd get back in touch. Mildred could wait because I didn't want her spoiling my evening. I got busy wiping off the kitchen counters, and then I set my dinner table.

I pulled the vacuum cleaner from its hiding place in my bedroom closet and hurriedly ran it over the floors, sucking up two weeks of grime. With that done, I stored my York barbells out of sight in the spare room that I'd never got around to furnishing. To let Tina see that I wasn't a slob, I hung out fresh towels in the bathroom.

Next, I hauled a chicken from my freezer and stuck it in the microwave to defrost. I cut up some lettuce and tossed a salad, being generous with the feta cheese, and placed two potatoes in the oven to bake. I've heard that people with social graces prefer wine at room temperature, but I like mine cold, so I laid the bottle in the refrigerator. After showering and splashing my face with smell-good lotion, I went to the Riverview Inn to get Tina.

She was waiting in her room and looked stunning when she opened her door. Her breasts were standing at attention under a reddish blouse, and she'd brushed her dark hair back under a blue knitted cap with just a tuft sticking out on her forehead. I felt like a teenager going to a high school prom as I walked her to my red pickup truck.

"They're stopping my project," Tina said as she got into the cab.

I turned toward her. "They've done what?"

"We must've created too much controversy, but my boss just said to wrap it up because we've exhausted our budget. They want me to put everything on hold until the next fiscal year."

"You just got started."

"It's not my decision to quit. Somebody with influence must've brought pressure at the top."

"You can't change their minds?"

"No, I don't think I can. Their decisions are set in stone."

She wasn't radiating warmth, and I realized this was not going to be a night for romance. I'd wine and dine her to the best of my ability, but I figured I was in for an evening of serious discussion.

We ate by candlelight and she sipped her wine slowly and took a forkful of my salad. She nibbled on a chicken thigh and smiled. "You are a man of surprises," she said. "Never would have guessed that you were such an excellent cook."

"Living alone inspires talent," I said. "But I do eat my share of quick fixes."

I told her not to, but she helped do the dishes, and afterwards we sat on my living room couch. I slid my arm around her shoulders and embraced her ever so gently. Her body tensed, but I saw promise in her eyes. As I held her, she turned her face toward mine. Our lips met softly, and she moistened my lips with the tip of her tongue. When we broke the kiss, I placed my hand on her breast, but she pushed it away. "Let's get to know each other better," she said. "Besides, it's time for me to get back to the motel."

Just before she closed her door at the motel, she teased me with a light brushing kiss and said good night.

CHAPTER
Twenty-One

I fell asleep thinking of Tina, but Joe Sacks initiated contact and there we were deep in VC territory at Ranger Compound Seven. I saw his hazy figure, clad in jungle khakis, wavering in a dark never-never land. Mines were blowing up, and through the streaks of flashing light, I saw Joe squatting in the bottom of a crater, stretching his hands toward me. His face was pleading and tortured, but he was just beyond my reach.

"Sarge, you've got to get my killer," he whispered. "I'll be stuck here forever if you don't. You're the only one left who can. Please . . ." I struggled trying to compose my thoughts, but he was gone in an instant. I forced open my eyes and felt my heart pounding, and I'd broken into a pissy-wet sweat.

"That damned war . . . ," I said to myself.

Sleep didn't come easy after that. My bed had turned hard as a pile of rocks and each time I turned over, it got harder. I tried to think of Tina again and wondered if Gloria had been right when she said that Tina was too young. Seventeen years' difference in our ages could pose a problem. Did I want to start a new family at my age? When I finally dozed off, the sun was bringing daylight over the mountain, and it was time to get up.

It took two mugs of coffee to wipe away the cobwebs. I switched my fretting to Riggins and realized that he might put me into a financial crisis. My checkbook wasn't healthy, and I'd find it tough meeting monthly payments if he suspended me. And I had no idea how I'd support my kids. My bank account totaled $187.29, but the county owed me another paycheck. The nest egg at the credit union would have to go for Frank Jr.'s teeth.

In the shower, I let the hot water run down my back but this time it wasn't relaxing. The phone buzzed, a reminder that I'd forgotten to set the answering machine, so I rushed from the john, dripping wet and dragging a towel. On the fourth ring, I picked up the receiver.

"When are you sending the money?" Mildred said. "Frank Jr. has his first appointment next week."

For a few seconds I didn't reply. "I've been very busy," I finally said. "I'll get the money there."

"When?"

"I'll try to mail it today. I'm caught up in two murder investigations, and I'm about to be suspended."

"You always did put your work ahead of your family."

I hung up and I didn't regret it. I flipped the switch on the answering machine so I could escape her if she called back. Then I returned to the shower and fumed about Mildred. It was like the old days. She was two hundred miles away in another state, yet she could still yank my chain.

I smeared a tablespoon of mayonnaise between two slices of bread and ate it before heading to the office. Frosty's cruiser was there, but I didn't see Riggins's Cherokee. That was encouraging, maybe I was getting a break. He couldn't suspend me without being there.

Frosty and I met on the courthouse steps and he shook his head very cautiously. "The boss ain't back, and I'm gonna be long gone when he gets here. You knew he'd blow up about you going to North Carolina without his okay."

I shrugged and went inside. Gloria greeted me with a nod but didn't speak. It was still mid-morning and I was pecking away on the old Underwood typewriter when Good Time called and wanted me to meet with him.

"We need to talk right away," Good Time said. "Come to the Apex parking lot and don't drive your cruiser." He hung up.

I borrowed Gloria's Chevy again, but this time I didn't promise to gas it up. I'd need every cent I had if Riggins suspended me, so I made a quick exit.

When I got there, Good Time ran from his old Cad and quickly jumped into the front seat of Gloria's Chevy. He directed me to park in a thicket behind his house where passing cars wouldn't notice us. "The word is that Toby Martin is out to get you. He thinks you killed Pete Dinkins and are framing Marvin Moore."

"You know me better than that."

"It ain't up to me to know or not know. If I can help it, I don't get mixed up in white men's business. Because you're my friend, I'm making an exception. That's how come I'm telling you."

"Somebody came to my place the other night. I must've scared them off. All they did was flatten the tires on my cruiser."

"You scared the hell out of 'em. From what I hear, they were fixing to burn you out. They heard something and ran off."

"Can you give me a name?"

"One was Harry Coltraine. The other was somebody he was out drinking with. Never did catch his name. They was after the thousand dollars Toby is offering for your dead ass."

"Damn, " I said. "Didn't know I was worth that much."

After I drove Good Time back to the Apex parking lot, I tried to picture Harry Coltraine. He was a local tough, I recalled, who hung around juke joints that played country rock, and he worked as a part-time bouncer at some of the places he patronized. His most serious brushes with the law had been for simple assault, but it sounded like he was about to graduate into the felony league.

I decided not to share this with Frosty as he was already on Riggins's shit list because of me. No use mentioning it to Hokie, either. He couldn't take action on my hearsay evidence.

When I got back, Gloria pointed to the sheriff's private office. "He's just got back and he wants to talk to you now."

I pushed open his door and saw him sitting in his chair and leaning forward with his elbows on his desk. He motioned and I sat in a chair directly across from him. "J.R. Taylor has filed a complaint against you."

"So I've heard."

"That's why I spent an extra day in Richmond. The attorney general is sending special agents here to investigate you. You've really embarrassed me."

I rubbed my head. "Have you talked with Hokie?"

"No, but I will."

"Have you already found me guilty of Taylor's charges?" I felt anger building up within me.

"Those agents will decide that as far as I'm concerned. But the idea of an investigation has shamed this department. As your boss, I'm doing my best to keep an open mind. I do know you went out of state without my permission and spent county money. You make it hard for me."

"I paid for my own lodging and I was on county business."

"Yeah. But you didn't have permission from Billy Bob or me to take your cruiser and bum the county's gas. That's why I'm suspending you without pay until further notice. Give me your badge and service revolver. I think you bought the shotgun with your own money. Is it in your cruiser?"

"No. I left it at home because it's ready for a cleaning. Am I suspended without pay?"

"Yeah," he said. "You left town without permission. That was the difference in being suspended with pay or without it. I'm putting Billy Bob Perkins in charge of your homicides."

"Billy Bob? He's never investigated a felony in his life, much less a murder."

"It's none of your business anymore. You're out of here until the AG makes a report."

I stood, gazing through his window overlooking the parking lot and the skyline beyond. The outside air was crisp and the snow had almost melted, leaving only patches on the shaded northern slopes. It was good hiking weather. I could make it home before the evening freeze, if I walked fast. I placed my .38 on his desk, along with my badge and car keys, and shoved them toward Riggins.

"I'll arrange for Billy Bob to drive you home," he said. "He should be here in a few minutes. You can bring him up-to-date on your investigations."

"The ride won't be necessary. I like walking on a cold day, and Billy Bob can come to my place and ask for information."

"But you're wearing my uniform. People seeing you walking like that will give my department a bad name. Could cost me votes."

"Kiss my ass," I said and slammed his office door. Gloria didn't look up as I stomped past her desk. She had warned me beforehand and I hadn't listened. Her silence probably showed good sense, because she was almost eligible to retire with full benefits.

In the corridor Billy Bob and I almost bumped into each other. His lanky frame bounced with each step. He was taking long strides, walking faster than usual. When he saw me, he grinned with his half-moon mouth.

"Frank, I didn't have nothing to do with the boss suspending you." His grin disappeared.

"How'd you know about it?"

"Me and the sheriff are family. I told him not to do this."

"You'll have fun working murder cases." I managed a smile. "It'll be good experience."

"Let me give you a ride. He told me he was taking your cruiser."

"He didn't just ground me," I said. "He castrated me."

"Don't blame me, I just work here. Let me give you a ride."

"I can walk."

I went home at a fast pace, talking to myself about the lack of support I'd gotten from Riggins. By fretting I made the journey easier, and I even turned down an offer of a ride from a passing motorist. Two hours later I got home and shucked my shoes and soaked my feet. The warm water felt good.

Once I relaxed, I thought about pumping iron because the blood rushing through my muscles unclouded my brain. I was about to load two heavy York plates on the bar and had a better idea. I poured myself a stiff drink and decided to pout. As I dallied with the glass of bourbon, letting it overtake me slowly, I remembered something. I'd forgotten to mail the money for Frank Jr.'s teeth, and this would give Mildred's present husband an opportunity to usurp my role as a father. I stomped across the room and unplugged the phone. I wasn't up to taking calls.

I took a look at my wardrobe and saw that I didn't have much to wear besides the brown uniforms. That reminded me that I had clothes to wash, so I gathered dirty laundry and stuffed it into the washing machine. The tub had filled with water when I heard a grinding noise and smelled the stink of scorched wiring. "You picked a fine time to break down," I said. By hand I wrung out the soggy mess and tossed it into the bathtub. Tomorrow, I'd go to the laundromat.

I wanted to call Tina at the Riverview Inn but didn't.

Before I got too drunk, I remembered Good Time's warning about there being a price on my head. I checked my shotgun and the Walther, making sure each had a full set of teeth. I went to the gun rack and loaded the other guns, a 30/30 and a 30.06 Remington. If Toby Martin or any of his henchmen came, they'd better bring body bags. Not everyone would be going home.

I dragged my chair next to a window and enjoyed the panoramic view overlooking the horizon while there was still daylight. As I looked, I regretted that the season was too cold for the buzzards to stage their aerial ballet. They circle elegantly, gliding with spread wings that play with the air currents. As the shadows fell, the distant mountains looked like low hanging clouds and the stars emerged to flicker and dance.

My trailer sits on a bluff that lets me view the valley below. I don't know how long I'd been watching when I saw headlights turning into my driveway. The car moved slowly as it came uphill and stopped at my front porch.

I stuck the Walther in my belt and hit the switch that turned on the floodlights. To my surprise, it was Tina. I watched her unravel her long legs and get out. She strolled leisurely to my front door carrying a tote bag. I slid the automatic into a drawer and clicked open the door.

"I tried calling," she said. "Nobody answered so I came to check on you."

"Unplugged the phone. Didn't need to answer a lot of calls."

"You made the six o'clock news again. Your suspension was Beth Sawyer's lead story. She interviewed Riggins and a lawyer named J.R. Taylor."

"What did they say?" I really didn't care.

"Riggins said you were off the payroll until the attorney general completed an investigation. Taylor blamed you for his client shooting a man."

"At least he didn't say I pulled the trigger."

"Might as well have. He claimed you'd threatened to kill his client. And he went on and on for a long time about police brutality."

"Did you know that a moonshiner has put a price on my head? I'm worth a thousand dollars dead."

"That wasn't in Beth's news report."

"Pete Dinkins, the man Marvin Moore shot, worked for him. He claims he's protecting his reputation."

"Does he really think you shot the man?"

"He must know better. I figure he's using this as a smoke screen to keep me from investigating Joe's murder."

She lifted her eyebrows. "I wonder if somebody isn't trying to run us both out of Ottway County."

"They'd be wasting their time on me," I said. "I'm not through by a long shot. I'll get the bastard who killed Joe Sacks, if I have to do it on my own."

"With you gone, who's investigating his murder now?"

I laughed. "Riggins reassigned both homicides to Billy Bob Perkins, his nephew."

"Will he help you?"

"Billy Bob is dumber than a bucket of rocks. He does well to endorse his paycheck. Riggins, in effect, has given up both investigations."

"I've found that ignorance begets ignorance. For some reason, the establishment fears smart people. It's always been that way."

"I'm still gonna get Joe's killer."

She took off her coat and carefully placed it on a hanger in my hall closet. Then she removed a bottle of wine from the tote bag. "I'm a girl. It's your job to uncork and pour the wine."

I dug out my corkscrew opener and twisted the top from the wine. Then I filled both of my two long-stemmed wineglasses about half full and handed her one. She smiled and asked me to propose a toast.

"Here's to our continued relationship," I said.

"A wonderful idea," she said. She wet her tongue in the wine, put the glass on the table, and came into my arms, pressing her head against my chest. I held her tight, and her body felt good against mine.

"Are you sure you have to go back to the motel tonight?"

"Not if you want me to stay. You shouldn't have to fight this alone. I feel partly responsible. You were protecting me when you got into the first shooting."

She got up and walked to my bookshelf against the dining room wall. After she brushed some dust from the covers, she said, "You and I like the same authors. John Donne, Rudyard Kipling, and Sir Walter Scott. The list goes on. Who is your favorite?"

"All of them," I said. "I'm a closet reader."

"Mary Mapes Dodge was my very favorite poet."

"She was an American," I said. "Among Americans, I like Poe and Sidney Lanier."

I warmed some leftovers, and as I fed her by candlelight, I recited Robert Service's "Shooting of Dangerous Dan McGrew," which I remembered from my army days. When I'd finished, she leaned across the table and kissed me lightly.

"I just saw a tenderness in you I hadn't seen before," she said. It looked like my luck had taken a turn for the better.

I leaned over to my tape player and searched for romantic music. All I had was bluegrass, so I didn't play anything. We sat on the sofa and exchanged soft kisses. I said, "Why don't you take off your shoes and get comfortable?"

She pointed to the tote bag. "I brought a change if you'll let me use your bedroom."

Tina surprised me when she came out, wearing a black nightgown edged with white lace. Its low cut exposed just enough flesh, and her body smelled like fresh mountain air, and I thought she was gorgeous.

"I took a chance bringing the gown. If you hadn't asked me—"

I took her into my arms and kissed her softly before she could say more. At first we kissed lightly, and gradually the kisses became more passionate. As I touched her breast, she massaged my body, and I led her to the bedroom. Our bodies blended and she sighed when I penetrated her. We moved in unison as if we were waltzing to the music of soft violins. I don't know how long it lasted, but when we were done, we both fell asleep. I was glad I had unplugged the telephone.

CHAPTER
Twenty-Two

At nine the next morning, I eased out of bed without waking Tina and tiptoed to the kitchen. I thought I'd surprise her with pancakes and opened a box of Hungry Jack mix. But she heard me stirring and called me back to bed, and in spite of the night we'd had, I found that with her I was up to the offer.

When I finally put the food on the table, I said, "My breakfast won't equal what you'd get at Maggie's."

"You are better than breakfast." She came across the room and planted a wet kiss on my lips as I stood in the middle of the floor.

"Do you have to go back to your office?" I asked.

"Yes, I do. Call me this afternoon at the health department. My reports are almost finished."

After we ate, I followed her out and we kissed beside her car in the cold morning air. I had a silly grin on my face as I watched her drive down the hill.

I phoned Hokie's office when she'd gone. His secretary told me he wasn't there and she didn't know when he'd be back. She recognized my voice, and I got the impression she was deliberately being grouchy. But I had too many problems to worry about her.

Then I remembered the broken washing machine. Sears covered it with a maintenance contract, but when I phoned, the Sears lady said they couldn't fix it until next week. I stuffed my dirty clothes into the Red Bullet and headed for a laundromat. While I was in town, I'd see if Hokie was back and later go to the credit union for the money to align Frank Jr.'s teeth.

I spotted a pickup truck lagging behind on my way to town. When I made a couple of side turns, the truck did, too. Whoever was following kept his distance. It could be hunters looking for the national forest, and it could be Santa Claus surveying rooftops. I had a hunch that it wasn't Santa. The Walther I'd put in the glove compartment made me feel comfortable. It was very effective at close range.

The truck still trailed as I passed Maggie's and continued across town. A red light caught the truck and I kept going. I proceeded for a mile or so until I reached Eubanks' Self Service Laundry, a one-story cinder-block building. Its white paint, which used to be bright, had faded. When the supermarkets moved to Burnsville, Henry Eubanks closed his neighborhood grocery and converted the building into a laundromat. Big bold lettering across its front plate window still advertised groceries. Heavy-duty washers and gas-fed dryers had replaced the rows of canned food and refrigerators filled with beer.

I got out of the Red Bullet and trudged inside, lugging an armful of dirty clothes. When I entered, Eubanks was collecting money from his machines, dropping the coins into a gallon bucket. He looked up and grinned when he saw me. "Glad to have police protection while I empty these coin boxes."

"I'm just a customer," I said. "I'm not police protection anymore. Sheriff Riggins suspended me until further notice."

"Suspended you for what?"

"The attorney general is investigating me."

Eubanks, a small man in his fifties with rosy cheeks, focused his deep-set narrow eyes on me. "Still, you wouldn't let anybody rob me, I don't think. We're lodge brothers. What happened?"

Without going into detail, I briefly outlined the chain of events. He said he hadn't been watching TV and this was news to him. "Sounds like Riggins overreacted. I'll give him a call and he'd better listen. He knows I swing a lot of votes. Never was overly fond of him since he gave me a lousy haircut when he was a barber."

I accompanied Eubanks to his car. "Got to get this money deposited before noon so the bank can post it. That means I get an extra day's interest. Doesn't sound like much unless you're a small businessman trying to make ends meet."

As he left, the pickup I'd seen following me was parked at the far end of the asphalt lot. Two men got out and walked in my direction. Neither carried a laundry bag, and I could sense in an instant that these guys didn't come to help me fold clothes. I went back inside and they followed.

Harry Coltraine swaggered up, rolling his beefy shoulders with each step. "Ain't got no badge to hide behind, have you? Without that gun you ain't so tough. I'm gonna kill your candy ass." He was big but had the kind of size that comes with drinking too much beer.

"You're the bastard who punctured my tires, aren't you?" I said as he whipped out a hawk-blade knife from under his jacket and started tossing it from hand to hand.

"Got your name on this blade," he said.

The second man was a dried-up twerp with a goat face and a purple nose. He stepped forward with his hand in his right pants pocket. "We were hid and saw you kiss that good-looking honey this morning. Too bad you ain't gonna see her no more." He drew a dinky little pistol from his pocket and pointed it at my head. I wouldn't have considered him a threat except for the gun, which did get my attention.

At that moment, Harry struck out with the knife and I forgot the twerp. The blade sliced through my jacket and nicked my arm enough to draw blood. I balanced on one foot and snapped a kick that caught Coltraine in his groin. He screamed, dropped the knife, and bent double like people always do when they're kicked in the balls.

I turned to face the twerp with the pistol. "That looks like a .22. Even if you're lucky enough to hit me, I won't go down. I'll get you in my hands and break your scrawny little neck. Then I'll stuff your body in a clothes dryer and let you roast. So make your play."

I started toward him, and he ran off still holding the pistol. The high heels on his cowboy boots clamored on the tile deck as he went for the door. I turned back to Coltraine, who had rolled onto his back. He was holding his balls with both hands and was screaming.

"Don't worry," I said. "You're not dying. Just wanted to make sure you wouldn't father any babies."

"Son of a bitch—"

I jerked him to his feet and slammed him against a wall. "The world doesn't need your kind polluting the atmosphere. Why are you bothering me?"

"Kiss my—"

I slapped him hard and a string of blood flowed from his nostrils. "You were right. I can't hide behind a badge now. This means I'm a civilian like you and there's nothing to say I can't stomp your rotten ass."

"You son of a—"

I slapped him again, this time on his right ear. "We'll start again with our conversation so you can be more civil. Next time, whatever I do will hurt more. Why are you after me?"

"Toby Martin," he said. "He says you shot Pete Dinkins over a load of liquor. He offered me a thousand bucks to do you in. Said he had to protect his reputation because Pete worked for him."

"You were gonna torch my home, weren't you?"

He hesitated and I shook him hard. "Yeah," he said. "But I wanted to flatten your tires first. That way you couldn't chase us if we woke you."

"Why didn't you finish the job?"

"Heard something like a window opening and we figured you'd shoot, so we took off."

"Do you own a black Dodge van?"

He shook his head. "I got that pickup outside and nothing else."

I grabbed his shirt. "Do you want me to hurt you more?"

"No. My balls are killing me. I'm sick on my stomach from it. I feel like throwing up."

"Let me ask you again about a black Dodge van. Who has one around here?"

"Honest to God. I don't know. Ain't seen one where I do my hanging out."

"Do you know who's been shooting at a lady taking water samples around Horse Heaven Mountain?"

"I swear I don't know nothing about that." He was almost crying. "I don't even own no gun."

"Who was the guy with the pistol?"

"His name is Tim Hawley. Met him at a joint over in Galax, and we've been running around together. He ain't local. He paints houses when he ain't drunk."

"You've got another thing to do before I let you go."

"Tell me quick, cause I got to get to the hospital. My balls are swelling."

"Tell Toby Martin not to fuck with me. He's pissed me off, and I'm not a nice guy when I'm pissed off. If he sends anybody else after me, he'd better hope they do the job. What's more, I don't want to hear of anybody else shooting at ladies. I don't have a badge so I don't have to go by rules."

"Let me go. I'm hurting bad."

"You tell them at the emergency room that you wrecked your truck. If you bother me anymore, it'll be a lot worse for you."

I released him and he stumbled toward the exit, half doubled over and moaning. He looked through the front window and turned back toward me. "Hawley stole my truck. It's gone. I don't have a ride to the hospital."

"Tough shit. Call a cab. There's a pay phone out front."

He hesitated. I swung the door open and shoved him out. He limped toward the pay phone, and I returned to the washers.

The dryers ate a handful of my quarters before my clothes were ready an hour later. As I started folding

laundry, Frosty surprised me with a visit and ambled back
to the table that I was using.

"Come to help me do laundry?"

"Naw," he said. "That women's work. I came to talk to
you."

"Not much I can say."

"Riggins was wrong. Told him so—and he put me on
probation. Me—with almost forty years of duty—and he
puts me on probation. Even told me not to talk to you.
What damned business is it of his who I talk to? Was
passing and saw the Red Bullet parked outside. He don't
get to tell me who I can talk to."

"Don't risk your job. He knows my truck, too."

"Listen, I've got my time made, and I can retire now
with as much take-home pay as I'm making. I'm hoping
Riggins will come to his senses."

"He doesn't like me."

"He's afraid because you're a professional and he's
not."

"When you came through the door, I thought Harry
Coltraine had taken out a warrant against me. Just beat the
shit out of him for pulling a knife. He nicked me on the arm
with it."

Frosty looked concerned. "How bad are you cut?"

"Not bad enough for stitches."

"Who's Harry Coltraine? Know most everybody in
Ottway County, but never heard of him."

"He belongs to the younger generation. Think he's the
one who flattened my tires. Hangs around joints and beats
up drunks. He and a twerp named Tim Hawley followed
me here this morning. They planned to finish me off.
Hawley had a pistol but didn't have the guts to use it."

"How bad did you hurt Coltraine?"

"Not too bad. Kicked him hard enough though. He
won't be chasing pussy tonight, or tomorrow night, either."

Frosty took a deep breath and sighed. "Billy Bob drove
out to my house asking for help. He's in over his head, and
wants you to help him."

"Has he come up with any new leads?" I knew that he hadn't.

"Nope. Riggins keeps pushing him for a progress report, and Billy Bob doesn't know what he's talking about."

"I'm not angry with Billy Bob," I said. "I'll try to guide him if he comes to my place, but he's got to get his own leads. I can't do that for him."

Frosty nodded. "He's lived out his fifty years dodging controversy. It's gonna be hard for him to start acting like a real cop."

"Have you seen Hokie anywhere?"

"Well, yes, but no. He's hiding in a motel room and drinking away his memories with 103 proof Fighting Cock bourbon. Nobody but me is supposed to know."

"How do you know?"

"Took him there but he doesn't want to be disturbed. His assistant is handling the District Court docket. Why do you want to see him?"

"Want him to get my pay restored. He said he was my lawyer."

Frosty nodded. "He ain't in no shape to talk now. Why not get an out-of-town lawyer and sue J.R. Taylor for slander? I saw him badmouth you last night on the evening news."

"Don't care about suing—only want my job and paycheck back. I've got obligations to meet."

Frosty said the state lab couldn't lift the serial number from Moore's pistol and had sent it to the ATF for further examination. I wasn't too concerned because I figured the gun would come back stolen anyhow.

He hung around making small talk while I finished folding clothes. "Don't worry," I said. "I won't tell Riggins you were here."

"Screw him," he said as he walked to his cruiser.

After I left, I stopped at the credit union, which was located in a doublewide near the courthouse. The girl behind the counter looked surprised as I entered. She turned her head to say something to another clerk, but caught my glare and changed her mind. I figured she'd seen J.R. Taylor on the evening news.

"They still let me come to town," I said. She made a weak attempt to smile.

Without further ado, I withdrew $3,000 and looked at the check with an ache in my gut. It'd taken me a long time to save that much, and now it was gone in one fell swoop.

"That leaves you with a balance of $284," she said.

"If you'll cash this check, it'll save me a trip to the bank."

She nodded and I endorsed the back of it. Then she gave me the money in hundred-dollar bills, and I stuffed them into my front pants pocket.

Next, I went to the post office and parked in a fifteen-minute space. I strolled inside, got a money order, and bought a priority mail envelope. My hand was nervous as I scribbled Mildred's post office box number at Charlotte, and enclosed the money order, along with three personal checks of twenty-five dollars each—Christmas presents for my children. Since I hadn't seen them for awhile, I just sent them money. Knowing that Mildred would open the envelope, I didn't seal it with a kiss.

"Want this delivered tomorrow," I said.

The postal clerk frowned. "You'll be lucky if it gets there in three days. Want to register it, too?"

"Yeah. Fix it so I'll get back a signed receipt. It's got to get there so my son doesn't spend the rest of his life looking like Ernest Borgnine."

The postal clerk shook his head and forced a smile. I figured he was too young to know Ernest Borgnine. After I paid him, he tossed the envelope into one of those special canvas pouches and turned his attention to a batch of junk mail.

I called Hokie from the pay phone inside the post office—in case he'd decided to get sober and return to work. His secretary said he wasn't there. She didn't elaborate, and her voice still was as cold as the mummies in Egypt. This time I understood why.

Out front one of the town's new cops was waiting for the meter flag to fall so he could slip a parking ticket under the Red Bullet's windshield wiper. I'd seen him on the pistol range and remembered that his name was Leonard Wren. He was so young looking that I thought he should be wearing a Boy Scout uniform.

"How much are you selling those tickets for?" I said to him.

He turned in surprise. "Didn't know this was yours. Anyhow, you weren't in there fifteen minutes. Sorry about what the sheriff did to you."

"Thanks."

"Did you know somebody stomped Harry Coltraine's ass?"

"No, who's Harry Coltraine?"

Wren shrugged. "One of our local toughs who pushes people he can whip. This time he picked a fight with the wrong guy."

"Really?"

"Yeah. Just came from the ER and he was in a lot of pain. But he's had that coming for a long time. His buddy told people at the poolroom that you kicked his butt, but old Harry claims he wrecked his truck."

"Don't believe I know Harry Coltraine."

After I departed, a passing van two blocks down the street suddenly caught my interest. It looked like the black Dodge from Old Train Lane. I stepped on the gas but the van was out of sight before I could negotiate the downtown traffic. Although I wasn't certain the van was the same one, I wanted to see if it had bullet holes in its back door.

I sped toward the Huckleberry Section, guessing that would be the van's destination. The gas gauge on the Red Bullet hovered near the empty mark, so I wheeled into a filling station for a pit-stop fill, but the archaic pump worked slowly.

Delaying me even further, the cashier fumbled and talked to herself as she counted my change. After I paid, I went south but the van was gone, and I had no idea where to search. I rode out the side roads between Burnsville and Horse Heaven Mountain. Nothing.

At Toby Martin's place, there was one car and Toby's pickup truck parked in the driveway. Then I drove to Sheppard's Store.

CHAPTER
Twenty-Three

At Sheppard's, the usual vehicles were parked out front, but the drivers had been careful not to block Elijah's gas pumps. The cars belonged to the daily regulars who hung out there. I got out of the Red Bullet and walked into the store.

Elijah was sitting on a three-legged stool and hunched over his desk scribbling on an invoice. He looked up and grinned.

"Ha, see where the sheriff canned you," he said. "Read this if you wanna know why I'm happy."

He handed me the latest edition of the *Burnsville Express*. An article in boldface type said that Riggins wanted the public to know he wasn't keeping a tainted deputy on his payroll. The bastard, I thought, sold me out for a self-serving front-page story.

"Don't think you'll be throwing your weight around anymore," Sheppard said. "Threatening me if I didn't tell you things—you had your nerve. What you got to say for yourself now?"

"Not a damned thing."

"Riggins says you're under investigation." Elijah was chuckling. "How does it feel not to be a big-shot deputy?"

I shrugged. "Don't feel any different. Badge or no badge, I'm gonna get Joe Sacks's killer. You can count on that. If I have to make a citizen's arrest, I'm putting his killer in jail."

"Why'd you come here?"

"To ask you a question."

"Okay. Ask. I might decide to answer."

"Has a black Dodge van been cruising the neighborhood?"

Elijah scratched his head. "Don't mind answering that one, because I haven't seen it. One of the mail carriers has a Ford Aerostar with four-wheel drive, but I don't know anything about a black Dodge van. Got any more questions?"

"One more."

He sighed and I knew he wanted me to leave. "Shoot."

"Heard anything new about the Sacks case?"

"The answer is no. Did hear he got a military burial in a VA cemetery over at Roanoke. At least the county taxpayers didn't have to buy him a plot."

As I walked out the door, he called after me. "Has Riggins appointed anybody to replace you? Nobody's been caught for breaking into my vending machine, and I expect some action."

"Call Billy Bob Perkins up in Gold Point. Far as I know, he's taking over my cases."

Outside, I saw Toby Martin standing next to the Red Bullet. He must have seen me pass his house and then followed. His overalls were stained with a grainy substance that I recognized either as hog feed or mash. When I walked out, he turned his head abruptly in my direction.

His pellet eyes stared and then he recognized me. He scowled and said something that I couldn't hear, and he started across the lot to his pickup.

"Looking for me?" I called out, but he kept going until he opened his cab door.

Then he faced me and yelled, "Better leave me alone. You ain't a deputy anymore. Got a right to defend myself if you bother me."

As I moved closer, he wiped snot from his nostrils with his shirtsleeve. "You've been wanting my ass and here I am," I said. He jumped into his truck and drove off without another word, but he looked back once in his mirror. I figured he didn't have a gun handy or he wouldn't have run.

I didn't follow him. He was probably hurrying home for a weapon, and I didn't need a shootout since I wasn't wearing a badge. I circled past Sacks's cabin and followed Old Train Lane through to Highway 21. On the way back, I got off the main highway and traveled a corkscrew dirt road running parallel with the highway. It was a waste of time because there was nothing in sight resembling the black van. I drove around until almost dark and all I saw was a handful of new dwellings cluttering the landscape.

"Too many flatlanders have discovered Ottway County," Frosty had said a few days earlier. "They won't be able to find jobs, and watch them get on our welfare rolls. Gonna run our taxes out of sight."

A woman, checking her mailbox adjacent to the road, threw up her hand and smiled as I passed. I waved back. At least she seemed friendly.

Back on Highway 21, a truck bearing Conrad DeWitte's logo was parked on the shoulder. A broken chain had spilled new-cut logs from a flatbed trailer, blocking the northbound lane. I pulled behind the truck and got out. The driver was waving a red handkerchief trying to direct passing cars around the mess. He was a stranger, but I saw that he was young and had long yellow hair tied into a ponytail.

"Can I help?" I said. "Don't have a cell phone, but I'll take you where you can make a call."

"No, don't need any help."

"Suit yourself," I said.

"Hey, aren't you the guy whose picture I saw on TV? You've got to be him." His words came through protruding buckteeth made more prominent by his lack of a chin.

"Suppose my picture gets around. Sure I can't help?"

"No. Another truck will be here in about thirty minutes." His pale blue eyes were glued to every move I made, and for a second I thought he might say thanks for stopping. He didn't.

No use telling him that DeWitte and I were friends and that was why I stopped in the first place. "What's your name?" I said.

He hesitated for a moment. "I'm Hamp Stallings."

"Live around here?"

"No."

"Knew I hadn't seen you before.

"I live over in Smyth County."

"You're alert to recognize me from a television picture."

"Er—I—watch TV every night. It's the only time I ever saw you, except now." I had a feeling that he was lying.

He still didn't say thanks for stopping, so I drove away wondering why he appeared hostile. To my knowledge, I'd never laid eyes on him before, but he surely was unfriendly over something.

In Burnsville, I bought two rib eyes that were on sale, but the butcher swore they'd be tender enough to cut with a fork. This time, I'd feed Tina American-style beef instead of Greek chicken. If she came, I'd be ready, and if she didn't come, I'd eat beef for two meals.

At my driveway entrance, fresh tire tracks alerted me that I had visitors, and I removed the Walther from the glove compartment. It was too early for Tina. As I came up the hill, I saw a dark Ford sedan parked at my trailer. It looked like a police car with the usual blackwall tires and no chrome. For some reason, cop types don't think they draw attention in plain black Fords.

One man sat behind the steering wheel, and his partner was standing outside smoking a cigarette. Both wore dark suits and hats, and looked like detectives from a Rex Stout mystery. The man inside had on a narrow-brim felt hat that accentuated his big ears.

"Are you taking a leak or looking for me?" I asked the man outside. He wore a white Stetson hat and a brass belt buckle shaped like a star.

He didn't answer, but walked toward the back of his car. He was in his forties, I guessed, and he had a dark pencil mustache. A bulge under his coat told me that he was packing heavy.

"I'm Ennis Maddrey," he said. "I'm a special agent with the attorney general's office." He handed me a card and it said that he was Ennis Maddrey. As I read it, he blew cigarette smoke through his nostrils and it floated upwards.

"Frank Stark," I said. "Been kinda expecting you."

Felt hat joined us. He was shorter but stocky like a pit bull. "This is Fentress Stell. He's a special agent, too," Maddrey said.

"I saw you standing outside and him sitting inside. He must not like secondhand cigarette smoke."

"I'm not here to make jokes," Stell said.

"You want to question me?" I had intended to talk to Hokie about this first, but he was incapacitated.

"Not now," he said. "This is a courtesy call, from one law enforcement officer to another. Just letting you know we'd be in the area asking questions and talking to people. Except for Christmas Day, we'll likely be here through the holidays."

"Sorry I can't ask you to a Christmas party, but I'm not entertaining this year," I said.

"Talked to Internal Affairs at the Charlotte PD," Maddrey said. "They said you had a hot temper, but you were honest. For the most part, they spoke well of you. Said you were a good street cop, but smacked the vice mayor's son."

"He was my ex-wife's second husband and whipped one of my kids. That's part of my life I choose to forget," I said.

"Cost you your job, didn't it?" Stell asked.

"They let me resign," I said. "Can I do anything to help you?"

"Not really," Maddrey said. "May need to interview you later. If so, I'll notify you. We might put on the polygraph." He didn't smile, letting me know that he was all business.

"Put me on now if you think I'm a liar."

"It's not that simple," Stell said. "But you know that. We'll advise you of your rights beforehand, if we think it's necessary. When we're done, Sheriff Riggins will be the first to get our findings."

"When do I get to know?"

"We assume Riggins will tell you right away," he said. "Another thing, a lawyer named J.R. Taylor thinks you might cause him harm. If anything happens to him, we'll be coming to see you."

They said no when I offered to brew coffee. We didn't shake hands and they left. I watched as their car went out of sight, glad that they were doing a prompt investigation. Hopefully they wouldn't hang me on Taylor's lies.

For a few minutes, I breathed the chilly mountain air and surveyed my kingdom. I had seven apple trees and three chestnuts, and all the black walnuts I wanted to pick up. My place was superior to any pad I could afford in a city. Come spring I'd have a field of golden daffodils that William Wordsworth could write a poem about.

I went inside and called Tina, and she answered on the second ring. "Want supper at my place tonight? The butcher swears the steaks are tender enough to cut with a fork."

"That would be great," she said. "I'm almost finished until after Christmas, and I was about to return to my apartment. I'll check out of the Riverview and head your way. It's time you learned that a New York girl can cook, too. While you pour the wine, I'll grill the steaks."

I drug out my vacuum cleaner again and started sweeping the floors. It always amazed me how quickly dust could collect at my place. While I was straightening up and stacking old newspapers, I came across a scrapbook in the bottom of a bookshelf. I pulled it out and then I remembered. It contained news clippings from the *Charlotte Observer*.

My picture, clipped from a front-page story, showed me receiving an award from the mayor when I was a beat cop. I'd rushed into a burning apartment building and rescued a child. This hadn't impressed Mildred, I recalled, for she went on vacation with her parents and missed the awards banquet.

I finished my housecleaning and put away the scrapbook. One way to chase off Tina, I figured, would be to bore her with talk about things that happened during my Charlotte years.

CHAPTER
Twenty-Four

This night I planned to relax and enjoy living for a change. Thanks to Riggins, the whole county could blow up and it'd be none of my concern. Riggins had Billy Bob to keep the peace, and I could have fun like it was a July vacation in December. And while I waited for Tina, I sat in my overstuffed chair looking at the skyline and for the first time in years began to appreciate the season.

My only concern about the suspension was that it'd hinder me in catching Joe's killer.

While I was pondering all those things, my door clicked open and closed without me as much as hearing it, and Tina appeared suddenly in the room beside me. She was carrying a shopping bag and wearing a red toboggan and dressed in a baggy sweatshirt.

"You look like an angel," I said.

"Maybe that's because I brought cheese and wine. Hope you like it."

"Are you kidding?" I said.

"Did I surprise you?"

"Yep, I was half asleep and daydreaming, Didn't hear you drive up."

"Perhaps I should've tooted the horn."

"I'd been so oblivious to the outside world that my mind wasn't in gear. That's not smart for somebody with a price on his head." I managed to push myself up and take the bag of groceries.

"We are spending Christmas together, aren't we?" she asked. "Looks like we're both alone, and I was wondering . . ."

"Wonderful," I said. "Where's your luggage?"

"In the car. Didn't bring it in until I was sure you wanted me."

"You have a standing invitation," I said, and a moment later I was lifting her suitcases from the trunk of her Escort.

Following the meal, Tina and I were sitting on the sofa making small talk over some brandy she had brought. A pair of headlights turned into my driveway and continued toward the trailer. I started to open the drawer and pick up the Walther, but I saw a shimmer of moonlight ricochet off a blue bubble, and realized this was a departmental call. The headlights stopped next to Tina's Escort.

I flipped on the outside light and saw Frosty sliding out from the driver's seat and Doc Lee getting out from the passenger side. I opened my door and told them to come in so they wouldn't freeze. Neither had on topcoats.

"Not my idea to come unannounced, but Frosty said you wouldn't mind," Doc said.

At that moment Frosty's eyes caught Tina standing by the refrigerator, sipping her brandy. "Excuse me," he said. He doffed his hat. "Hope we're not interrupting anything."

"Would you like coffee, tea, or something stronger?" Tina asked.

"Coffee would be fine for me," Frosty said.

Doc frowned. "I'll take some hot tea if you have it. Frank and I have business to discuss, and a cup of tea might help me explain things clearer."

"Want me to go into another room?" Tina asked.

"Won't be necessary," Doc said. "Expect Frank's brought you up-to-date on his affairs. The county's in a sad mess without him. Adam Riggins is coming out in the morning to offer Frank his job back."

"Are you a spokesman for Riggins now?" I asked.

"Hell no," Doc said. "I'm here because Ottway County needs you."

"Come back for my sake," Frosty said. "If we have bad trouble, I'm the only one available. Together we make a team. Can't do it by myself. Too damned old."

"You mean you need my muscle power," I said. "You want me to wrestle the Saturday night drunks to the ground."

"That's only part of it," Frosty said. "We also need you to help us get our reports right. I can't do paperwork."

"Riggins was a real asshole," I said.

"I don't care about Riggins," Doc said. "For all I care, he can go back to cutting hair. People here need you. Riggins came to my house this evening because he couldn't find Hokie. He asked me to come and ask you to take your badge back."

"It might be that I don't want it."

"You're too mature to be proud," Doc said. "How're you going to make house payments?"

"It's not that," I said. "Two special agents from the AG's office are in the county now asking questions. They might have an opinion. I'd like a letter of clearance from them before going back. If he wanted, Riggins could reinstate my pay."

"A clearance letter is only a piece of paper," Doc said. "Shouldn't have anything to do with what Riggins does. He answers to the people of this county and not the attorney general. Unless you come back, we're without adequate law enforcement."

It was not an easy decision to make at that moment, but I did need my paycheck. "I'll consider it, but I make no promises."

"Let Riggins eat crow but take the job back," Frosty said. "Ten more years and you can retire and sit up here and pick apples."

I nodded. "I'll think about it."

After they'd gone, Tina said, "Are you sure about Frosty?"

"What about him?" I said.

"He's unnerving—the way his eyes followed me—like he was undressing me."

"He was undressing you. Most women say he has X-ray eyes," I said.

"Hope he isn't dangerous. I mean—is he okay?"

"Sure. Just say no and he'll go away. Some women, like the county administrator's secretary, lead him on to watch him make a fool out of himself."

"But he's so old."

"So's George Foreman, but he still packs a wallop."

She sat on the sofa and snuggled up to me. I put my arm around her and drew her closer. "Why don't you go back to school and get a master's degree? Then you could teach criminal justice at the state academy," she said.

"I'd like to do that, but I have to support three kids who carry my name."

"I was fortunate not to have children during my four years of marriage."

"You were smart," I said. "Now you don't have to worry about straightening crooked teeth."

She arched her eyebrows and gave me a puzzled look. I explained to her about Frank Jr. not wanting to took like Ernest Borgnine, and that it was costing me three thousand dollars with no guarantee that he'd someday be president of the National Rifle Association.

"You see, I wanted children but my husband didn't," she said. "I still love him, but he placed his career first."

"He must be in law enforcement."

"Not at all. He has an accounting degree, but he makes his living painting pictures."

"He's an artist?"

"Yes, and he's very talented. Won blue ribbons in juried shows all over and in Europe, too. One of his landscapes hangs in the governor's mansion at Richmond. The networks have covered his showings."

I shrugged. "I thought it would be tough making a living painting pictures."

"Not if you're Lamar Jordan."

"Your ex-husband is Lamar Jordan?" Anybody who watches public television has seen him display his wet-on-wet techniques. He slaps on paint like he was doing a picket fence, but somehow he has more fun than Tom Sawyer and gets beautifully realistic landscapes.

"Worked two jobs to help him through school," she said. "That was when he wanted to be a CPA. Then his art career took off and he became famous. Despite his fame, he's the kindest person I know. I wish we could have made our marriage go, but it just didn't work out. There wasn't another woman or another man involved. What about your marriage?"

"We split," I said, "because we were not compatible. She's married twice since. Our divorce wasn't easy and it cost me my job. I was unemployed long enough to start chasing my last dollar. It wasn't fun. I drifted up here and Riggins hired me."

"How did you find Ottway County?"

"I was born here," I said. "Had an uncle who left me this place, along with a mortgage. He'd worked in the mines and bought it with the idea of building a house. Never did, though, because he died first of black lung disease. I was overseas at the time."

"It's good that you still have contact with your kids, even if it is expensive."

"Yep. Every time my ex thinks of a new way to draw blood, she calls."

After a few minutes and another sip of brandy, she changed the subject. "Tell me about Joe Sacks. He must've been a special person for you to care so much."

"He saved my ass in Nam. Stayed at the top of a bunker fighting even after they'd almost shot off his pitching arm. The Cobra gun ships rescued us, and he was later flown out. I'd forgotten he was from these parts until I spotted him one Monday morning walking across the courthouse parking lot. It was raining, but he recognized me right off. I'd driven him home and on the way, we talked about that damned war."

"That explains why you are so determined to catch his murderer."

"Joe didn't deserve to die like that."

She saw my eyes had filled and kissed me on the cheek. "What do you tell Riggins if he comes out tomorrow?"

"I don't know. We'll wait and see."

CHAPTER
Twenty-Five

John Donne's busy old sun didn't get his chance to rouse me the next morning. After a night of lovemaking followed by deep sleep, Tina and I heard a banging at my front door. I struggled to my feet, reaching for a robe that I'd thrown across the foot of my bed. I squinted at the lighted wall clock. It was ten minutes after six, not even daylight. Tina yawned and began to stir.

"Who is it?" she whispered.

"Might be the sheriff."

"Why so early?"

"He's got a one-track mind and no manners."

My guess was correct. Adam Riggins stood shivering in the morning cold and doffed his hat when I opened the door. The subfreezing temperature had hunched his shoulders and drawn his head into his topcoat.

"May I come in?" he asked.

I nodded and stepped aside. He went straight to a heater vent blowing hot air, cupped his hands, and began rubbing them together. "Took you a long time to come to the door. I thought I was gonna freeze out there."

"I was trying to sleep."

"Called Paul Simmons," Riggins said. "Told him I'd made a mistake and shouldn't have suspended you. I told him you were reinstated. Also, them two agents from Richmond said it looked like you hadn't done nothing wrong and that lawyer Taylor was wasting their time."

"What did Simmons say?"

"Said I shouldn't have suspended you in the first place."

"Why did you? You hit me hard at Christmas time."

"You shoulda let me know you were going to North Carolina."

"You were gone and it wasn't a wasted trip. I found that Marvin Moore's a certified nut."

Riggins handed me my badge. "Your gun is out in my car."

"Why not reinstate me after Christmas? Then I can enjoy the holiday for a change."

He shook his head. "You need to come back now. Elijah Sheppard is in the hospital. Somebody's beaten him 'bout to death. He's too scared to make a statement, but I figured he might talk to you."

"What happened?"

"Don't know for certain," Riggins said. "A customer found him unconscious at his store. I don't think it was a robbery or anything like that. He may have a skull fracture, and they don't know what else. They're talking about transferring him to a regional hospital."

"Who did it?"

"He won't say," Riggins said. "Said he didn't want his store burned down. The customer who found him called 911."

"Are you sure it wasn't a robbery?"

"No. I can't find Frosty, and Billy Bob didn't want to answer the call alone."

"You mean nobody's been out there?"

"Nobody's been there," Riggins said. "I talked with Elijah's wife, and she says she'll run the business for now."

"Where's my cruiser?"

"Billy Bob's waiting to bring it soon as I call him."

"Has he come up with anything in the Sacks case?"

"Billy Bob don't do well talking to people about serious business."

"I'd better see Elijah right away," I said. "He could die or they might move him. Then it'd be a lot harder for us to interview him."

"Do me a favor, will you?" Riggins said.

"What?"

"Call Henry Eubanks at the laundromat and tell him I've reinstated you. He's called me twice about your suspension, and that man swings a bunch of votes."

"Let him sleep for a while, I'll see that he gets the word."

Riggins started out but stopped before he got to the door. "I know tomorrow is Christmas, but could you stop by the office and do our monthly stats? I'll get Gloria to type it up so we can get it in the mail."

"I'll do it the day after Christmas. Won't be anybody working in Richmond until then anyhow."

"If you need me, I'll be in the office for awhile," Riggins said. "Beth Sawyer of Channel Three is gonna meet me there at nine."

"What's she doing here?"

"Don't worry, she's not after you. She's doing a story on how well we feed our prisoners on Christmas Day."

"Be careful around that woman," I said. "She may be sneaking up for an interview with Marvin Moore."

He nodded. "I hadn't thought about that."

After Riggins brought my .38 and left, I walked into the adjacent kitchen and put on the coffee maker. I heard water running and figured Tina was taking a shower. I was glad she'd stayed in the background during Riggins's visit. If he'd noticed her Escort parked outside, he hadn't mentioned it. When she came out, I'd have her a mug of coffee poured.

I snapped on the radio, hoping to get a weather report. After scanning the dial, I got an AM station airing UPI's morning news. The top story was about the Federal Reserve Bank and the bullish stock market that had been helped by a late splurge of Christmas buying. They quoted a source close to the president. He said the market was in good shape. Not a word about the weather in Ottway County.

Tina ambled into the kitchen wearing a pinkish terry cloth robe. Her shiny black hair was wet and fanned out across her shoulders. I poured us both a mug of coffee. We went into the living room and sat on the sofa. "I heard you talking to Riggins," she said, toying with her mug. "Did he reinstate you?"

"Handed me my badge."

"Did you accept it?"

"I did. It'll give me my best shot at catching Joe's killer."

"It's a shame you have to work for somebody like that."

"Nobody else made an offer, and I can use the pay."

"When do you go back on duty?"

"Billy Bob is bringing my cruiser now. I have to drop him off at the courthouse and go to the hospital."

"You're going today?"

"Yes. Somebody beat up Elijah Sheppard, the postmaster in the Huckleberry Section."

"We had plans. Couldn't it wait till after Christmas?"

"They're talking about transferring Elijah to another hospital. If they do, it'll make it harder for me to see him."

"Does he connect to everything else that's been happening?"

"Elijah knows more than he told me," I said. "Maybe he'll talk now."

She sipped more coffee, but remained quiet while I waited for Billy Bob to arrive. I kissed her lightly on the cheek as I left. "I promise to hurry," I said. "I'll leave my Walther for you just in case. Don't let anybody come in and shoot if they insist."

CHAPTER
Twenty-Six

The warm afternoon temperatures had melted most of the snow and our chance was gone for a white Christmas. As I drove to the hospital, I took the main drag through the business district and saw Christmas decorations everywhere. They were suspended from utility poles and glistening in store windows. This prompted me to buy Tina a gift. Perhaps a piece of jewelry, I thought, but my wallet wasn't bulging with cash. I'd shop for something nice but inexpensive, and maybe I'd get lucky.

About a half dozen people sat in the hospital's waiting room, where dull gray drapes hung from a long row of windows. Rays of sunlight gleamed through, exposing floating dust motes in the air. A young man in GI fatigues sat on a couch next to a yellow-haired girl. His arm was around her shoulder. An older woman was watching television. Regis and Kathie Lee were interviewing some fat guy with a white beard dressed in a red suit. Nobody looked my way as I stepped up to the information desk. The pink lady didn't notice me until I cleared my throat. She was wrapping a Christmas box.

"What room is Elijah Sheppard in?" I asked.

She quit wrapping the box and checked the computer. "He's in three-one-three," she said. "I'm surprised he's still here. It looks like they're trying to send everybody home for Christmas."

I smiled, thanked her, and headed for the elevator. It dropped me off on the third floor where the strong smell of disinfectant reminded me of a freshly scrubbed jail. People in white were busy in the corridors and at the nursing station. A man passed me pushing a cart stacked with metal breakfast trays. I cleared my throat, but a nurse carrying a clipboard ambulated past without so much as a glance. Another nurse—one I recognized—-sat in a straight-back chair behind a row of computer monitors. She was shuffling through a stack of papers on her desk, but she looked up and our eyes locked. "Frank, what brings you to our madhouse?"

"Came to see Elijah Sheppard."

"He's in room three-one-three. But you'd better hurry because we're transferring him to Lewis-Gale Hospital at Salem."

"Is he hurt that bad?"

"Don't think so," she said. "His doctor wants a scan that we can't do here."

I hurried to his room. Elijah managed a painful frown and blinked at me through swollen eyes as I approached his bed. They'd shaven his head and slapped a bandage on the back of his skull where he'd been whacked. His face looked too small for his long nose that was inflated to twice its normal size, and had already turned purple. He pushed a button, cranking his bed to a sitting position.

"Thought the sheriff fired you." He spoke in a hoarse whisper.

"Got reinstated. Ottway County can't function without my services. Came especially to see that big Band-Aid on your head."

"Got nothing to say. You can leave right now."

"Not until we talk."

"Not making any statement. Somebody already thinks I'm your snitch."

"Who?"

"Not saying. I don't want more trouble."

"Seems to me you've already got trouble. You're not letting somebody get away with this, are you?"

He shifted his eyes upward to the ceiling and didn't answer.

"Somebody hurt you and that's a crime committed in my district, and that makes it my business. If it happened at your store, it's also a federal violation since you're the postmaster."

He clinched his hands together and said, "Just get out of here."

"Nope," I said. "No way am I overlooking it. If I have to, I'll question everybody in Huckleberry."

"You're causing me trouble. Leave me alone."

"Was it Toby Martin? He saw me leaving your store."

I saw fear blossom in his eyes and he sucked on his lower lip. "Er—ah—don't say nothing to him."

"If he did it, sign a complaint. I'll put him behind bars."

"I'm not saying nothing."

"Are you afraid of him?"

"You'd be, too, if you had any sense. He's dangerous. You can't put him so far behind bars that he can't get out."

"He did this to you, didn't he?"

"I'm not talking and I'm not signing any complaint. If you arrest him I won't testify, so you might as well leave me alone. Just leave." His voice quivered and I could see his body trembling, so I didn't push him more.

Roberta Sheppard was waiting in the hall. She was a short thick woman with a double chin and looked like she could cook biscuits. "Mr. Stark," she said, "put Toby Martin in jail for what he done to my husband."

"Did you see him do it?"

"No. If I had, I'd sign a warrant."

"Did Elijah tell you Toby assaulted him?"

"He won't talk, but I know. Toby did it out of plain old meanness."

"I need a witness who's willing to testify. Can't convict him otherwise. Are you positive you didn't see anything?"

"Yes, I wasn't there when it happened. It's going to be hard for me to run the store with Elijah laid up. Thank goodness we've delivered most of the Christmas mail."

"I'll do what I can," I said. I pulled a notepad from my shirt pocket, jotted down my home phone number, and gave it to her. "Call me if you learn anything."

Roberta hesitated. "There is one thing. May not have anything to do with what you're investigating. But people who come to the store are talking about big trucks riding through our area during the night."

"Might be trucks picking up milk from dairy farms, but I'll check into it," I said.

Before I left the hospital, I used one of the staff phones and called Gloria. I didn't want police scanners hearing that I planned to confront Toby Martin, and Elijah's assault gave me cause to do that. If Gloria could get up with Frosty, I wanted him to come along. Otherwise, I'd accept whoever was available, except Riggins's reserves.

Frosty wasn't answering his radio, so Gloria called his home. His wife didn't know where he'd gone and wasn't expecting him until supper. Riggins, Gloria said, also was out of pocket. After he'd met Beth Sawyer, he and his wife drove to Gold Point for a visit with Billy Bob's family. That left me with no choice but to make the trip alone.

I stopped on Main Street at a jewelry store and bought Tina a necklace made with imitation pearls. Then I went to a florist next door and bought her a dozen red roses. It sounded corny but I wrote on the card, "Your luv is like a red rose."

The florist gift-wrapped both the roses and the necklace, and when she'd finished, I drove south on Highway 21 toward Toby Martin's place. I turned onto a curvy blacktop road and followed it for four or five miles until I reached Martin's driveway. He'd pushed too far by attacking Elijah, and he was still my number-one suspect in Joe's death. Deep down I hoped he'd break bad so I could adjust his attitude.

His driveway was slick with the kind of traffic bootleggers and whores get—lots of muddy tracks all stopping at his front porch. The pickup truck he usually drove was gone, but a car was there. I maneuvered up the path and parked close to his house. Nobody was in sight, so I slid out slowly. Smoke was rising from the chimney, and blaring country-rock music seeped through the unpainted clapboard walls. I stepped onto the front porch, knocked twice on his door, and stepped aside in case of gunshots.

A scraggy woman with blotchy skin cracked open the door and squinted at me through pink-veined gray eyes. Her apron was smudged with food, and dried snuff caked her lips. She examined me for a few seconds before stepping onto the planked porch. She was too ugly to be a whore, so I knew Toby's traffic came from selling either moonshine or dope.

"Is Toby here?" I asked.

"No," she said. "I'm Martha, his wife." Her hair was pulled straight back and knotted at the back of her head. Old scar tissue above both of her eyes showed that Toby had left his marks. She didn't invite me inside.

"Do you know where he is?"

Martha shook her head. "He left in his pickup truck and took his chainsaw. I'd say he's cutting stove wood."

"How long has he been gone?"

"More than two hours. Ought to be back soon."

I saw the curtains part at a window beside the front door. At first I thought it was Toby, but I was wrong. A tall, skinny boy of about fourteen pushed through the door and came out. "If you're looking for him," said the boy, "he's probably down on Miller's Creek. That's where he generally gets wood." The boy stuttered badly. His left arm rested in a homemade sling and his face was bruised.

"Hurt yourself?" I asked.

"Yes sir," he said. "That's why I'm not helping saw wood. My arm must be broke. It hurts awful bad."

"Been to a doctor?"

"No, Mama's been soaking it in turpentine."

"Now, you be quiet and get back in the house," Martha said.

"I hurt, Mama. I need to see a doctor this time."

"What happened?" I asked.

"You shut up and get in the house," the woman said, narrowing her eyes at me. "He fell down the steps bringing in a bucket of water."

"Is that so?" I said to the boy.

He didn't reply but looked at his mother.

"Toby's not here and I'd appreciate it if you'd leave," she said.

"What's your name?" I said to the boy.

"Rodney, but folks call me Buddy."

Fire danced in Martha's eyes. "I'm asking you again to please go."

I looked at the boy. "Do you want me to take you to the emergency room?"

"Don't have money for that," she said.

"Social Services will probably help."

"I'm scared to go," Rodney said. "I'd get another whipping if I did."

"Toby says we don't take charity," Martha said. She put an arm around the boy's shoulder and pushed him back into the house. Then she slammed the door.

I sucked in a deep breath through my nostrils as I walked back to the cruiser, trying to pick up the sweet odor of fermenting mash. One whiff and I'd have probable cause for a search warrant. But all I smelled was the stench from Toby's hog pen.

I headed toward Miller's Creek and turned onto an unnamed gravel road running parallel with the stream. If his son told me the truth, I ought to be able to see where he turned into the woods.

CHAPTER
Twenty-Seven

I didn't travel very far before I found tracks going into the woods on a barely passable dirt trail that abutted and ran next to Miller's Creek. The treads looked like the knobby prints I'd seen in Toby's yard. The old logging path was in bad shape. When my cruiser began to drag bottom, I parked and walked about three or four hundred yards to a shallow ford. That was where the knobby tracks had recently crossed the creek.

I heard a chainsaw and assumed that Toby was about a quarter mile beyond the crossing. If I waited, he'd likely return this way when he finished loading. I trudged back to the cruiser and sat. Occasionally, the chainsaw stopped and I heard thumping sounds when he tossed wood onto the truck's bed. No need to worry about hunters because the saw's noise would chase off any game in the area.

An hour later, I heard Toby coming out. His pickup truck splashed through the creek and came banging over the humps in my direction. My cruiser blocked the path, and he stopped about twenty yards away.

The pickup truck was weighted down and sitting low. Toby's chainsaw sat on top of the load of black locust wood. With his hands clutching the steering wheel, Toby looked over his shoulder at his empty rifle rack. He glared at me with the most hate I'd ever seen. I watched him, ready to shoot if he reached for a concealed gun. He didn't, so I marched up and yanked open his truck door.

"Get out, and keep your hands where I can see them."

At first he didn't budge—just stared at me with those hateful eyes.

"Am I going to have to drag you out?" I said. "That can be done."

He slowly released his grip on the steering wheel but took his time getting out, keeping his hands away from his pockets. He was muscularly built and of medium height. "You gonna shoot me like you did Dinkins?" he asked.

"You got the wrong information." My adrenaline was fired up, and I was hoping he'd break bad.

"Everybody knows you want to kill me, just like you did Dinkins." Toby curled his mouth into a sneer.

"I didn't shoot Dinkins. Who told you that?"

His eyes avoided direct contact with mine, and he was silent for a few seconds before answering. "Everybody knows it."

"Is that why you beat up Elijah Sheppard?"

"What are you talking about?"

"I'm talking about you almost killing Elijah Sheppard."

He drew a breath and snorted, and when he exhaled, it smelled like pig shit. I was glad when he turned his head and looked toward the skeleton of a dead chestnut tree. He rubbed his hands together and said, "Elijah tell you that?"

"It doesn't matter who told me. You're in real trouble like you've never seen before. You don't beat up a postmaster. That can get you federal time at Marion, Illinois, and you won't be boss of the walk there. Better pack your suitcase for a long stay away from home."

"I'm not admitting nothing."

"I know you put a price on my head and sent two punks after me. But they both had a yellow streak and weren't tough enough to complete the job."

"I ain't talking about that either," he said.

"You deny that you sent Harry Coltraine and Tim Hawley to kill me?"

"I might have said something to them at the poolroom, but I'd have come myself if I wanted you dead." He puffed his cheeks and clinched his fists. I felt like he was trying to build enough courage to try me.

"You're lying."

He shrugged. "You can't prove it."

"You're in deep trouble, and anything you do bad is gonna make it worse."

He was silent again as he glanced at the dead chestnut. Water gushing over rocks in the creek provided the only sound until he spoke. "I've heard about you, Deputy Stark. You put out the word that you're gonna kill me because you think I shot Joe Sacks."

"Did you?"

"Hell no. I hardly knew that old drunk. Saw him a few times at Sheppard's Store. Didn't even know where he lived."

"Don't believe you."

"I don't give a damn. I'm telling you the truth. Don't have no reason to lie. Didn't have nothing to do with his death."

"Who did?"

He shrugged. "Don't know nothing about that."

"Why did you beat up Elijah?"

"Ain't making no statement that can be used against me. Why do you want me dead? I didn't kill Sacks."

"Who said that I wanted you dead?"

"Different people. They say you killed Pete Dinkins to get even with me. Now, they say, you're framing Marvin Moore for it." I saw sweat drops popping out on his forehead, and he was breathing faster. He'd lost the courage he'd tried to build up, and I figured this conversation had gone further than he wanted.

"Who's putting out this shit?"

"A truck driver for one."

"What truck driver?"

"Don't know his name. He stopped at Marvin's the day before Dinkins got killed. I was there getting a Coke."

"He tell you this?"

"He warned me and Marvin to watch our asses."

"Sure you don't know him?"

"He was young and was driving a flatbed, hauling logs. I know he wasn't lying because you want me so bad you got Elijah Sheppard pimping for you."

"Why should you care about Elijah?"

"I don't, but I saw you at his store in that red pickup."

"I reckon you'll deny breaking your son's arm?"

Toby's expression was one of unexpected shock. "He's a damned liar if he said I did. Him and my old lady had better not been talking to you."

"Are you making a threat?"

"Am I what?"

"Making a threat," I said. "If so, I'm gonna arrest you right now."

He didn't reply but picked at his nose with his little finger. I figured he was weighing the odds, so I raised the ante. "If I do arrest you, you'd better hope I don't find a gun. That'd be possession of a firearm by a convicted felon and would guarantee you jail time."

"Don't take me in." He lowered his voice. "My family needs this firewood."

By backing down, I guessed that he didn't want to be searched. His expressed concern for his family was bullshit. You don't break your son's arm if you're a concerned father.

"Will you take your boy to the hospital emergency room? His arm needs tending."

"That ain't none of your—"

"That's my offer. Take it or leave it." I stepped toward him.

"All right," he said. "I'll unload the wood and take him to town."

"Be sure you do, because I'll be checking with the hospital."

Without turning my back, I got into my cruiser and drove to Burnsville.

CHAPTER
Twenty-Eight

When I reached town, I went to the sheriff's office for the first time since Riggins had suspended me. I pulled out the latest edition of the Virginia code from my desk and reviewed the section pertaining to assault charges.

"Your return postponed my retirement," Gloria said. "And before you ask, you don't have any messages."

"How'd you know that was coming next?"

"Because you're a creature of habit. You always ask that. Billy Bob scribbled some notes I typed, but they don't say anything new." She handed me a typed sheet of paper with Billy Bob's signature at the bottom.

I studied his notes for a second, shook my head, and trashed them. Then I looked at Gloria. "If I didn't come back, you were gonna quit?"

"Oh yes," she answered. "I'm old enough and I've got the years in to do what I please. How was your short vacation?"

"Not much happened except I thought I spotted the black van going through town."

"Did you find it?"

"No. Just got a quick glimpse and it was gone. Believe it went toward Huckleberry."

"While I think of it, Beth Sawyer is looking for you. The sheriff told her you were back on the job and hot on the trail of Sacks's killer."

"Thanks," I said. "She's the last person I want to see."

"She may call you at home. Your telephone number is published."

"Hope she doesn't," I said. "I don't have anything to tell her."

"Maybe she has a crush on you."

I frowned. "That's why she crucified me on the air."

"Paul Simmons wasn't very kind."

"He just printed the facts," I said. "Didn't go way off in yaw-yaw land speculating about what might have happened."

After I thumbed through the mail in my basket, I waved my hand at Gloria and left the office. I passed Conrad DeWitte and Skeeter Dobson talking in the lobby in front of the courtroom. Both turned simultaneously as I marched past. I would have liked to have asked DeWitte about his truck driver, the one Toby had mentioned. But definitely not in the presence of Skeeter. I'd catch him another time when we were alone. So I nodded and wished them a merry Christmas, and kept going.

The parking lot was empty, and I strode quickly to my cruiser. I didn't want Beth Sawyer running up and ambushing me with questions.

As I headed home, I entered into a dialogue with myself about my relationship with Tina and wondered where we were going. What if she wanted to marry and have children? I asked myself. I'd decided that I was too old to start a new family.

Tina, wearing a navy blue blouse, kissed me on the lips when I got home. She'd decorated the living room, and the place actually looked like Christmas. "I wish we had a fireplace where we could hang our stockings," I said as I handed her her present. She took it and gave me a neatly wrapped package.

"Can I open it now?" I asked.

"You better not—or you won't have a surprise tomorrow."

We sat close on the couch, and her hair smelled like fresh-cut flowers. Perhaps I would like to start a new family with her.

"How was the assault victim you went to see?" she wanted to know.

"He'll make it. I drove out to Huckleberry and had a prayer session with Toby Martin. He's the one who beat up

Elijah and may have had something to do with Joe's murder."

"What did Martin have to say?"

"Said he would take his teenage son to the hospital. The bastard's a wife beater who broke his own son's arm."

"People like that shouldn't have families," she said.

"Beth Sawyer was looking for me at the courthouse, and I got away without seeing her," I said. "That damned woman—"

"Probably she's after your body," Tina said.

"I do have a nice body. That's why so many girls knock at my door."

"You don't believe me?"

I shook my head. "Beth Sawyer would sleep with the devil for a news scoop."

"She'll try to seduce you," Tina said. "Then you'll tell her everything."

I laughed. "She'd be wasting her time, because I don't know everything."

She thought for a moment and said, "You could tell her about Toby Martin abusing his family."

"Everybody already knows that. It wouldn't be news."

"At least you may have gotten his son medical attention."

"Not sure," I said. "I'll check with the hospital in the morning. I don't think that he'll run his still right away. Unless he's got it hidden well, he'll let that mash rot and set up later at another location. He's paranoid, and he'll be seeing me behind every bush. I've blown my chances of catching him stirring mash, at least for the time being."

"Why does he object to me taking water samples?" she said. "I wasn't interfering with his business."

I scratched my ear and thought for an instant. "I'm not absolutely positive that he knew about the men in the black van. This is bigger than Toby. Except for Dinkins, I haven't identified anyone else working for him. He did prod a couple of bastards to come after me, but they weren't regular employees. Toby's mean and his ass ought to be in jail, but he's not all that smart. I need to subpoena his long-distance telephone calls. It might give us a clue if somebody away from here is talking to him."

"You're saying those men in the van didn't work for him?"

"It doesn't look like it. Nobody I know has seen the van close to his house. I've looked several times and it hasn't been there."

"How do you suppose he's involved?"

"Right now I'm not sure he is. No doubt he's making moonshine liquor. I'm certain he assaulted Elijah Sheppard, but I don't know how he ties in with the van. He said a truck driver warned him that I was planning to kill him."

"Do you think he really got such a warning?"

"Not sure," I said. "When I asked him to identify the driver, he claimed he didn't know his name."

"Got any idea who it would be?"

"Only a hunch. One of DeWitte's trucks was broken down beside Highway 21. I talked to the driver, and he did fit the description Toby gave me."

"Why not ask DeWitte about him?"

"Haven't had a chance. He and Skeeter Dobson, the court clerk, were talking when I left the courthouse. I'd rather meet with DeWitte at his office where we can talk in private. Skeeter runs his mouth too much."

She toyed with a glass of Merlot while I continued talking. "I hope Toby takes his son to the emergency room. Maybe they'll call Social Services and somebody will sign a warrant."

Tina showed me that a New York girl could cook. She grilled our steaks, baked a couple of big Idaho potatoes, and threw together a tossed salad that was delicious. I enjoyed every morsel.

We turned in early. She brought her body close to mine. As I stroked her soft breasts, I felt her body stiffen. We kissed, but I noticed a coolness that hadn't been there before. I perceived that something was wrong, something I didn't understand. I almost asked her about it but didn't, not certain that I wanted to know the answer.

The phone awoke me. I'd forgotten to switch on the machine, so I picked up on the fourth ring. It was the town police department. I needed to go to the hospital. There had been a shooting in the Huckleberry Section, and Toby Martin was dead. Doc Lee wanted me to come right away. A 12-gauge shotgun blast had ripped off the side of Martin's head.

"What's happened?" Tina asked.

"Somebody shot Toby Martin."

"Is he badly hurt?"

"He's dead. Doc Lee wants me to meet him at the hospital. He's already called Adam Riggins."

.

CHAPTER
Twenty-Nine

I beat Riggins to the hospital. Doc was sitting at his desk in the basement dictating into a machine, and he swiveled around when I entered his office. "Damned medical records people want my notes pronto. It's the paper pushers and insurance companies running things now."

"What about Toby Martin?" I asked.

"Got exactly what he had coming," Doc said. "He was beating his son, and his wife picked up a shotgun and pulled both triggers. Killed him instantly with his own shotgun."

"When did it happen?"

"About three hours ago."

"Nobody called me."

"Nobody knew it until the ambulance brought him here."

"Was the boy hurt?"

"He's a patient up on the third floor. Toby broke the boy's nose and was kicking him when his wife let him have it. They've got her under sedation in the psychiatric unit. I tried to interview her, but she was babbling wildly. She did admit the shooting. Said it was to save her son."

"Hope they X-ray his arm," I said. "He was holding it in a homemade sling when I was at his house earlier."

"I'll advise orthopedics in the morning."

"What were you able to find out?"

"The mother dialed 911 to get help for her son. She never mentioned that she'd shot her husband and that he was lying dead on the floor. The EMTs found her in a daze when they arrived. The boy lay on the floor unconscious. They brought the woman and boy to the hospital and called another unit to fetch Martin's body. I told them to bring the shotgun."

"Where's the weapon?"

"Got it tagged in my evidence locker. Can't do much in the way of ballistics with a shotgun. I've got the names of the EMTs for you."

"Is the boy able to talk?"

"See him tomorrow," Doc said. "He's in right much pain."

"Has anybody made arrangements for feeding the livestock out there?"

"Yes. One of the EMTs knows Toby's brother-in-law. Said he'd get in touch with him."

Adam Riggins appeared. The ceiling lights magnified his tightly drawn monochrome pallid skin and wild spiked hair. His pouchy eyes squinted at me, and I knew the shooting had interrupted his sleep. It was the first time I'd seen him so rumpled.

"We've got to go to Toby Martin's house to do the crime scene," I said. "You and I are the only ones available. Since it's a fatality, I suppose Doc will want to come along, too. Martin is dead. I'll explain on the way out."

Riggins didn't argue, just shrugged and looked at Doc. "Hope the television cameras aren't around. I look like a mess."

"You surely do," Doc said. "Zipper up your pants. For a neatnik, you look terrible. I've done autopsies on better-looking bodies."

Riggins fished in his shirt pocket for a Tampa Nugget that he jammed into his mouth unlit.

Doc and Riggins followed me down the deserted hall. I'd parked in a slot next to the front entrance, away from the ER. Unless it's business, I avoid emergency rooms, even when they're empty.

"At least we'll get to search Toby's premises," I said as we drove south.

"What is there to find?" Riggins asked. "Martin's dead. You can't charge a dead man."

"So's Dinkins dead," I said. "If we're lucky, we might find the black van. Maybe it's stashed in one of the outbuildings. We still haven't solved Joe Sacks's murder."

Thirty minutes later, I pulled up to Martin's house. It was dark except for a mercury vapor light out front ricocheting its bluish glow. It didn't penetrate far beyond the front steps, so I stopped the car, rolled down the windows, and listened. A grim silence hung in the night air. Sporadic clanks from Toby's automatic hog feeder broke the hush.

"Are you sure this is the place?" Riggins asked.

"Yes, I was here this afternoon."

After listening for a few seconds, I pulled the cruiser closer to the house. No lights shone through the windows, so I handed Doc and Riggins spare flashlights that I kept in the trunk. I smelled fumes from a dying fire that I assumed was coming from the chimney. I got out quietly, but Riggins slammed his door.

The front entrance was standing ajar, so I stepped inside, switched on the lights, and looked around. One deep breath and I smelled the blood. I followed its odor to the kitchen where the linoleum floor and the walls were splattered red. I saw heel marks where the EMTs had apparently dragged Martin while stuffing him in a body bag. Some of the shot had missed and punched holes in the refrigerator.

"Damn," said Riggins. "Never seen nothing like this."

In another room, I looked into a closet and found a box of twelve-gauge No. 6 shells. I also found three pistols, another shotgun, and a military surplus .30/06. None were the right caliber to have killed Sacks. I tagged them and toted them to my cruiser, where I retrieved my camera.

A half-full urinal under the bed and a stack of filthy clothing on the floor made the main bedroom stink. I fanned through discarded paper bags and envelopes but found nothing of value. Most of the mail was utility bills from the electric power company. There were telephone bills, but no toll calls.

I searched for a specimen of Toby's handwriting to compare with the anonymous letter sent to Paul Simmons about me. Apparently, he didn't do any writing.

His son's bed was in a room not much bigger than a large closet, and it consisted of a straw tick mattress spread across empty soft-drink crates. Seeing a straw mattress brought back boyhood memories to me.

"This is a nasty house," Riggins said. "Don't look like the dishes have been washed in a week."

I shrugged. "Go in the bedroom and whiff that piss pot."

Doc grinned. "Adam, you should watch me do autopsies. It would strengthen your stomach."

Riggins put his hand over his mouth. His eyes bulged and pasty face turned green. For a second, I thought he was going to puke, but he didn't.

"You guys finish up here," I said. "I'm going to check his outbuildings behind the house."

I found his still in what had once been a chicken house. He'd scattered straw across his yard to camouflage the traffic. When I swung open the door, the odor of ripe mash hit me smack in the face. I counted nine one-hundred-gallon wooden hogsheads that he'd neatly lined up in a row. He'd packed hog manure next to the barrels so the heat would make the mash work faster. A dead rat was floating in one vat.

He had a bottled-gas cooker beneath a hundred-gallon copper still and a dozen upright tanks of propane. To get water, he'd extended a hose from his well. Empty hundred-pound sugar bags littered the dirt floor. One glance told me that Toby had been operating this outfit for a long time. I looked but I saw nothing to show that he'd been processing marijuana. Nor did I see the black van.

"I see why he had his hog pen so close," I told Riggins. "The hogs ate the spent mash and eliminated any runoff problems. He didn't have to worry about Tina Jordan's water samples giving him away. The stench from his pigs covered up the mash scent. That's why I couldn't smell it when I was here."

"How're we gonna tear up this mess?" Riggins wasn't interested in my explanations. "We can't blow up his building, can we?"

"No," I said. "Looks like we've got a lot of chopping to do. Why not call your reserve deputies? They could get investigative experience."

Riggins nodded and asked me to go back into the house with him. He used Toby's phone to wake up his reserves. "Make sure you bring your axes when you come," he told them.

CHAPTER
Thirty

I was dead tired when I got home just before sunrise on Christmas Day. Tina was asleep on my bed, so I kicked out of my shoes, undressed and stretched out on the sofa with a blanket. That way I wouldn't disturb her. My triceps ached from chopping those mash barrels. I'd done most of the work when we destroyed Toby's still, and my undershirt was drenched with sweat. To keep the noise down, I didn't jump into the shower. That could wait until later. Sleep came easy, and I didn't fight any wars or have bad dreams.

Tina woke me at noon with a kiss and a mug of freshly brewed coffee. "Our Christmas turkey is out of the oven and it's waiting for you to carve it," she said. I followed her into the kitchen and sliced the turkey, and then dug the cork from a bottle of red wine. She'd set an appetizing table, and after I gave thanks we ate.

When we'd finished, we went back into the living room and opened our presents. She held up the necklace and smiled, saying that it would match her blue blouse. Leaning forward, she kissed me softly. I then unwrapped her gift and found a corded bolo tie with a star—something she hadn't bought at a bargain counter.

"You can wear that when you make detective," she said.

I shook my head. "We don't have detectives in Ottway County. Don't even have sergeants or lieutenants."

She cleaned the kitchen and put away leftovers while I showered. Afterwards, we sat on the sofa and I put my arm around her shoulder, pulling her close. I caressed her and teased her lips with light kisses. Then I kissed the soft part of her neck and pulled her even closer. Although she went with me to the bedroom, there was a slight chill in her responses that I hadn't felt before.

Long ago in Nam, I'd learned to respect my premonitions, and more than once this had saved my platoon from ambushes. And the inkling I had about Tina's coolness had been right, too, I discovered later in the evening. She told me she was going to Blacksburg but would try to come back for New Year's Eve.

"Thought you were spending the week with me. I'm disappointed that you're not," I said.

"You've got so much to do with your job that you won't miss me. I've got office work to do and plenty of housekeeping chores at my apartment."

Just before sunset she kissed me lightly but without the previous passion. And then she was gone.

I was sitting by my window gazing at the horizon when the phone buzzed. I snatched up the receiver on the third ring, and it was Frank Jr. calling from Charlotte. "Merry Christmas and thanks for the money, Dad," he said. "I hope I'm on my way to a career that will make you proud."

"Hear DePaul has a good basketball team. Are you going to play for them?"

"Dad, I won't have time to play sports because I've got to devote all of my energy to my acting classes. I thought making all-state in high school would satisfy you."

I meditated on that one before answering. "Whatever you do," I finally said, "be the best that you can be. I love you, son. " His call made me feel better.

The next morning my place seemed lonesome without Tina. I put a pan of water on the burner and made instant coffee. As I sipped the coffee, I wondered if Tina was coming back. I missed her.

Then I drove down Main Street to the office of the *Burnsville Express*, located in a building that once housed a department store. I wanted that unsigned letter to the editor Simmons had shown me. The handwriting might be valuable if I could find a match.

Simmons was bent over his desk scribbling on a pad with a big yellow pencil. He swiveled his head when I entered. "What brings such a famous investigator to my humble office? Are you here to see me edit copy from my rural correspondents?"

"I want that unsigned letter to the editor you showed me."

"Already threw it away," Simmons said. "Why did you want it?"

"For comparison. I might get lucky and find a handwriting sample that'll match it."

"Even if I had it, I wouldn't let you have it under those circumstances," he said. "A good newsman protects his source."

I frowned. "It wasn't a source. It was a lie. You didn't even have a name to go with it."

He shook his head. "Nevertheless, that's the way it is— thirty—which means the end to old-time reporters. So don't ask me any more questions about that letter."

Next I drove north toward the town's new industrial park and stopped at DeWitte's shiny office building. I pulled into a parking space reserved for visitors, yawned, and rubbed my eyes before getting out. I was still tired.

DeWitte had built his two-story structure out of granite his trucks hauled eighty miles from Mt. Airy, North Carolina. "This building will anchor a new beginning for Burnsville," he'd said four years ago at the ribbon-cutting ceremony attended by the lieutenant governor.

The architect had been generous in blending glass and marble with the granite, giving it an upbeat look. Like DeWitte himself, this building looked like a symbol of the future. His logo was carved into a bronzed plaque attached on the front of the building.

For the first time in fifty years, the Virginia State Lodge had selected a Burnsville man to be grand master, and he was Conrad DeWitte. I saw that as a tremendous honor for a small town in Southwestern Virginia.

I hadn't bothered calling Riggins before my visit, although I knew that he and DeWitte were hunting buddies. I pushed through the double glass entrance and faced Conrad's receptionist, a petite young girl with fiery hair and dancing blue eyes that reflected the color of the morning sky. She looked up from her desk and flashed me a pleasant smile.

I smiled back. "May I see Mr. DeWitte? I don't have an appointment, but it's important."

"Have a seat and I'll call his secretary. I think he's here but he might not be. Sometimes he leaves by the back door." She was cheerful, and I sat down.

In a few seconds DeWitte appeared, and I got up. We shook hands as lodge brothers and he motioned for me to follow. We walked down a hallway on dazzling white tile and past a water cooler, and then went up a short flight of stairs. His office was spacious with expensive furnishings. He invited me to sit, and I eased myself into a leather armchair with a fat bottom.

"Glad you stopped in." His voice was resonant and distinct—the same as when he spoke in public. "How can I help you?" He rubbed back his salt-and-pepper hair with his hands. "I have an appointment in a few minutes, but I always have time for a lodge brother, especially one who's an officer of the law."

"I understand," I said. "Need to find one of your drivers. He's young, blond and wears his hair in a ponytail. Believe his name is Hamp Stallings."

DeWitte knitted his brows and thought for a moment. "Not sure he's still with us. He's the driver who told me about the Orange Fix-It Shop being a bootleg joint. I passed on his information to you and Deputy Johnson."

"Toby Martin told me this guy said bad things about me. That's why I want to talk to him."

"He said bad things about you?" DeWitte wrinkled his brow.

"Said I planned to kill Toby. It was the same lie that caused J. R. Taylor to ask the attorney general to investigate me. I'm trying to find out who started that crap."

"I'm shocked that Stallings would say such a thing. My employees certainly should know I don't stand for that kind of behavior. Have you and Stallings had trouble?"

"No. I offered to help him the other day when he lost his load of logs on the highway. Far as I know, that's the only time I ever met him."

"Where's this Toby Martin?"

"Dead. His wife killed him last night. I talked to him yesterday afternoon before his wife pulled the trigger."

DeWitte raised his bushy gray eyebrows. "He's dead?"

"Yes sir. Shotgun blast ripped off the side of his head."

"Think he could have murdered our brother, Joe Sacks?"

"I'm not sure. That's why I want to talk with Stallings to see if he can shed some light on this."

"Wait a minute, and let me see if he's on the payroll." He picked up a phone and punched in some numbers. "Come to my office. A police officer is asking about Hamp Stallings."

In a few minutes, a huge man with a swarthy complexion came through the door. I guessed him to be at least two inches taller than me and he must've weighed three hundred pounds, but he moved with the agility of a cat. He laid a black ledger book on DeWitte's desk and flipped through its pages with huge hairy hands. "I've got the company roster—"

"Deputy Stark wants to know about Hamp Stallings," DeWitte said. "Do we still have him on the payroll?"

"No sir. We let him go." His voice was heavy with a crisp Northern accent.

DeWitte looked at me. "This is Jake Monsure, my operations manager."

Monsure was younger than me and had long, dangling arms. He offered his hand and we shook, but not as lodge brothers. I felt strength in his bearlike grip, and I knew he wasn't a candy ass. "You must be new in Burnsville," I said. "Haven't seen you before."

"Imported him from New Jersey," DeWitte said. "Used to play pro football until he hurt his knee. Hasn't moved his family down yet." DeWitte invited Monsure to sit in a leather chair across from me. Since I didn't follow pro football, his name didn't register.

Monsure shrugged. "The boss keeps me busy. I tend to the shop while he's away."

"Got any idea where I can locate Stallings?"

Monsure rubbed his square forehead with the back of his hand. "I paid him and he left." He opened the ledger and turned some pages. "He lived in Smyth County, but I think he may have a room somewhere here in town, too. Don't know where, and I don't have a phone number for him. I did hear he was moving to Kentucky."

"How long has he been gone?"

Monsure frowned. "I fired him before Christmas. We don't allow drinking on the job, and he'd been stopping at a bootleg joint south of town."

"With insurance rates already too high, we can't allow drinking and driving," DeWitte said. "If you find Stallings, I'd like to know why he was talking about you. You don't seem convinced that Martin murdered Sacks?"

"No," I said. "Toby was mean enough, but I'm not sure."

"Have you found out who shot at that girl?"

"Nothing new has turned up," I said. I didn't tell him about the black van. I wasn't even sure that the one I'd seen in town was the same vehicle.

We sat in silence for a few seconds. DeWitte folded his hands over a stack of papers, and we exchanged glances and he looked at his Rolex. He was sending me a signal to say something or leave. I didn't blame him.

Finally, I broke the silence. "If you'll give me Stallings's last address, I'll be on my way."

Monsure picked up a memo pad on DeWitte's desk. He opened the black ledger and wrote on the pad with a ballpoint pen. He tore off the page and handed it to DeWitte, who glanced at it, and passed it to me.

"Don't think you'll find him," Monsure said. "I'll ask around and maybe come up with where he's living now. Some of my crew might know. It'll be next week though. We've shut down for the holidays except for a skeleton crew."

I thanked him and looked at the piece of paper. As I rose to leave, DeWitte pushed his chair back and started to get up. "Keep your seat," I said. "I'll show myself out."

Since my hopes of interviewing Stallings had fizzled, I thought about visiting Moore at the jail. He might talk now that he'd been shut up for a few days. If he remembered Stallings's conversation with Martin, I would know that Toby had been telling the truth. But I couldn't interview Moore without his lawyer's consent or I'd break rules that would jeopardize our case. Chances that Taylor would cooperate were slim—even slimmer if I requested it.

As commonwealth attorney, maybe Hokie could pressure Taylor into a little cooperation. I keyed the mike and asked Gloria to find Hokie. She told me right off that he was having a conference with two agents from the AG's office.

CHAPTER
Thirty-One

With Gloria's help, I made contact with both Hokie and Riggins, and asked them to meet me in the sheriff's private office. I asked Gloria to hold all phone calls and to keep anyone from disturbing us. Toby's death had stalemated my investigation, and I figured that it was time to make something happen.

"This case needs to be pushed ahead or it's gonna die," I told them.

Riggins blinked but kept quiet.

"How are you going to make it move?" Hokie said.

"By interviewing Moore," I said. "Maybe I can shake something loose."

Hokie shook his head. "Are you serious? Taylor wouldn't allow him to talk with an officer, particularly you."

"You can talk to J.R. and convince him that I might be able to help his client."

Hokie shook his head again. "I'd be telling him a lie. Nothing will help Moore. I've charged him with first-degree murder. Hell, he's facing a death sentence."

"Not if I come up with extenuating circumstances," I said. "If he told me something that would help his case, I'd pass it on to you. You could then tell J.R."

"What do you have in mind?"

"Toby claimed a truck driver, who'd stopped at the Orange Fix-It Shop, warned him that I was going to kill him the first chance I got. If Moore heard this, being paranoid and all, he may have been prodded into firing his pistol at us. With his mental condition, Taylor might be able to use that and save his client from the death penalty."

"Did you get a name for the truck driver?" Hokie said.

"I think I did. He's Hamp Stallings, and he lives in Smyth County."

"Talked to him yet?"

"Not yet. He worked for DeWitte, but Conrad's manager fired him for drinking on the job. Moore could move us forward if he'd talk. Paranoid or not, I need to interview him."

"They haven't had him examined to see if he's paranoid," Hokie said.

"My interview could give them a good reason to call for one."

"It'll never work." Riggins broke his silence. "I say let Moore get the hot seat. Who cares about him anyhow?"

"His grandmother down in North Carolina," I said.

Hokie frowned. "The system cares, too. He's a human being."

"So was Joe Sacks," Riggins said.

"Moore isn't charged with killing Sacks." Hokie's face had reddened. "He's charged with killing Pete Dinkins and shooting at Frank Stark and Frosty Johnson."

"Will you talk to J. R. and get me permission to speak with Moore?" I said.

"Not promising any results," Hokie said, "but I'll give it a try."

I pushed myself out of my chair. "Let me know what he says. I'm driving over to Smyth County and see if I can locate Stallings. DeWitte's operations manager thinks he may have moved to Kentucky. If so, maybe I can find out where in Kentucky."

"I'll let the sheriff there know you're coming," Riggins said. "He's president of the state sheriffs' association, and I don't want to piss him off by going into his jurisdiction unannounced."

Frosty was hunched over his desk filling out returns on papers he'd served when I left Riggins's office. He frowned at me critically through his half-sized dime-store reading glasses.

"Have a good Christmas?" I asked.

"Good as could be expected," he said. "Would have been better without all this paperwork you left me to do."

"Tried to contact you. You missed the excitement. Toby Martin got killed and we found his—"

"Heard all about it. You call chopping mash barrels excitement?"

I grinned. "Beats serving all those papers. Want to ride with me to Smyth County?"

Frosty shook his head. "Got too much to do to play with you today."

In a way, I was glad to be going alone. I was blue as a full moon over Tina's departure because her presence had brightened my outlook on everything. Losing her for a few days made my heart heavy. The drive to Smyth County would give me an opportunity to scrutinize our relationship. Maybe she didn't like being left by herself at my trailer while I went off playing detective.

The address I had for Stallings led to an old two-story gabled house surrounded by evergreen shrubs that needed trimming. It sat in an oak grove between Marion and Seven Mile Ford, and across from a truck stop that had been abandoned when a new I-81 rerouted nearly all of the commercial traffic.

I knocked at a door with a sign saying "Office," and a plump little woman of about forty came out, peering at my badge and uniform. She didn't answer right away when I asked if Stallings lived there. After a moment or so, she said, "He rents an apartment from me, but I haven't seen him for a few days. He wasn't here during Christmas."

"Did he tell you where he was going?"

"Nope. Is he in some kind of trouble? I never knew him to drink or cause problems."

"He doesn't drink?" I raised my eyebrows.

"Nope. I would have seen his empty beer cans or whatever when I carried out his trash. He lives by himself and is really quiet."

"Does he have family that you know about?"

"He moved here last summer from the coal fields in Wise County. He may have kin over there. Only time I talked to him was when he paid his rent, and he always paid me on time."

"Do you have a key for his place?"

She thought for awhile and pursed her lips. "Sure, but should we go into his apartment? His rent is paid up for another week."

"Let's make sure he's not lying in there dead. It would smell up your place. Better we take a peek."

She made a face, and dandruff fell on her dark sweater when she brushed back her hair. "Guess you're right. I don't want no dead man stinking up my apartments. It'd run my other tenants off." She removed a key from a ring and handed it to me.

When I unlocked his door, I concluded that Stallings hadn't moved away. If he had, he'd left a lot of clothing behind. His shirts and trousers still hung on hangers in his closet, and his dresser drawers were stuffed with socks and underwear. Two empty suitcases were under his double iron-frame bed. On top of his dresser, he had a quart fruit jar half filled with quarters. I found an unopened half-gallon of milk, some Cokes and a loaf of bread in his refrigerator. The date on the milk was good for three more days.

"The local sheriff's department may send a deputy out here to talk to you," I said. "We may have a missing person."

She shook her head from side to side, making the dandruff look like snowflakes. "Run a good place here. Never had any trouble with the law, and I don't want none now."

I gave her one of my cards and asked her to call collect if he came back. She said she would. I thanked her and headed for the Smyth County sheriff's office in Marion. The sheriff was mildly curious as to why I'd come to his county. Riggins had called but didn't tell him I was investigating a murder. I filled him in on what I figured he needed to know and told him Stallings may be missing.

He shook his head. "He's a grown man. I don't have enough help to keep tabs on everybody. If we come across anything, I'll call. By the way, you had a call from Burnsville. They want you to go to the commonwealth attorney's office. Said it was important."

CHAPTER
Thirty-Two

The drive back took an hour and gave me time to wonder why Stallings would get fired for drinking at work when his landlady described him as a teetotaler. This didn't make sense. A man who drinks himself out of a job would leave dead soldiers lying around his living quarters, I figured.

Hokie was waiting for me in his outer office with the good news. "I talked to J. R., and he's agreed to let Moore tell us what he knows."

"That's great," I said.

"But there's a catch. He insists on being present during the interview. I told him that was okay. He's waiting for me to call him back."

Taylor met us on the courthouse steps and shook hands with Hokie. My feelings weren't hurt when he deliberately ignored my presence. We'd clashed too many times to be friends.

"I'm trusting you not to take advantage of my generosity," he said. "Remember, I'm allowing this interview with the understanding that I can stop it anytime I think my client is incriminating himself."

Hokie nodded. "Wouldn't have it any other way. J. R., my word is my bond. Frankly, you have everything to gain since Moore is facing the death penalty."

The three of us stepped into the elevator, and I punched the third-floor button that took us up to the jail. A trusty whom I had booked for being drunk in public was wringing out a mop in a bucket. He grinned when he saw me. "Beats sleeping under bridges," he said. "You did me a favor, except I sure miss an occasional snort."

Since there was no interview room, Jud Peele, the jailer, escorted us to his office. He grabbed the end of a scarred wooden table and dragged it to the middle of the room. Next, he opened a closet and pulled out four folding chairs and carefully positioned them around the table. By then perspiration rings had mushroomed from under his arms, and he was puffing. "It's hell being this fat," he said.

We sat and he left. Five minutes later he brought Moore into the room. "Be still while I take these cuffs off," Peele told the prisoner. The obese jailer dwarfed Moore, who was of medium height and skinny. Moore had shaved the dark stubble from his face and looked almost boyish. He had on a fresh blue denim shirt that was unbuttoned at the collar, but he smelled like jailhouse disinfectant when he slumped into the chair the jailer had provided.

"Anybody got a cigarette?" His hands had a bad case of the shakes.

"Sorry," I said, "I don't smoke."

Taylor, who had taken a seat next to him, fished around inside his coat pocket and came out with a pack of Winstons. He handed the pack to Moore, who yanked one out. Taylor snapped his lighter and lit the cigarette. Moore inhaled deeply and blew curly slithers of smoke upward. "Been dying for a smoke."

He blinked his tiny eyes and squirmed while he surveyed his surroundings. I guessed that he would try to escape if the opportunity came. Peele was too fat to catch him if he did. Moore sat there shifting his eyes like a trapped rat.

"These people want to ask you some questions," J. R. said. "Answer them if you can, but don't tell them something you don't know."

"Talked to your grandmother," I said. "She's worried about you."

Mentioning her helped dissipate a little of his wildness. He looked me squarely in the face. "Is she okay?"

"Doing fine," I said. "Just worried about you."

"Wouldn't be here if I'd listened to her."

"Have they put you back on your medication?"

"Yes, but I don't need it."

I looked at Taylor. He nodded and wrote on a notepad.

"What do you want me to say?" Moore asked.

"Do you remember Hamp Stallings coming to your place? He drove a flatbed tractor-trailer."

"Blond guy with long hair?"

"That's the one. He wore it tied up in a ponytail."

"Yeah, but I never did know his name. He always drank diet 7-Ups."

"No alcohol?"

Taylor objected to my question. "Don't answer that. You're trying to get my client to admit he sold liquor."

Moore frowned. "I did sell liquor. Everybody knows that. But the guy he's asking about always drank plain 7-Up."

"Remember seeing him talking to Toby Martin?"

"Sure do. He told Toby you were going to kill him the first chance you got because you thought he shot your friend. Said that you'd blow me away, too. It scared hell out of me. Never heard of cops shooting people they didn't like."

"Was he alone when he stopped in?"

"Mostly. One time two guys met him there. They didn't buy anything. Talked to him and left."

"What did they talk about?"

"Didn't listen. Besides, they were almost whispering."

"What about these two guys? Can you describe them?"

"It was awhile ago. Can't remember too much what they looked like."

"Try to," I said. "Were they old or young?"

"I ain't good on guessing ages. They were big men, I remember that. One had a beard."

"What were they driving?"

He frowned for a minute. "They were in a van, I think. I didn't pay much attention when I found out they weren't cops."

"Did you get a look at the van?"

"It was dark, could have been black."

"Could you identify them if I showed you pictures?"

"No. I don't think I could."

"You shot at the officers," Taylor said, "because you thought they'd come to kill you, isn't that right?"

"Yes sir, that's right."

We finished the interview, and the jailer led Moore out. Taylor looked at Hokie. "I take it that you noticed my client is not mentally competent."

"Prepare an order for the Circuit Court judge to sign," Hokie said. "I won't oppose him being evaluated."

I walked Hokie back to his office. "He's telling the truth," I said. "What he told us coincides with Toby's story. Why would somebody be out to set me up?"

"Don't know, unless it was to divert suspicion. What's your next move?"

"Going back to Horse Heaven Mountain. This time I'll do a thorough search. No more drive-through stuff. Gonna walk every step of the way to Highway 21. Maybe we've missed signs we shoulda seen."

"Don't try it alone," Hokie said. "I'm calling Riggins to insist that he get you help—even if he has to call the state police. Whatever's out there, it's bigger than we thought and could tie in with those men shooting at Tina Jordan."

"At least Toby Martin isn't a suspect now."

CHAPTER
Thirty-Three

Beth Sawyer waved when I stepped through the front door of the courthouse. A short-legged man with square shoulders was with her. He was loaded down with a video camera that looked too cumbersome for easy handling. She approached me with her spiked heels tapping like machine-gun fire.

At that moment, Skeeter Dobson stepped into the foyer and diverted her attention long enough for me to escape. She stopped to chat, and I bounded up the stairs to the sanctuary of the sheriff's office. Gloria was playing solitaire on the computer screen next to the radio panel.

"Already worked the crossword?" I said.

"It was easy today." She looked in my direction. "Those two state agents from the attorney general's office are in there meeting with the sheriff." She pointed toward a closed door leading into Riggins's office.

"Am I invited to the party?" I said.

"No," she said. "Riggins doesn't want to be disturbed."

"How long have they been here?"

"At least thirty minutes, maybe more."

I nodded, sat at my desk, and thumbed through an accumulation of paperwork, dispensing with what I could. As I ripped open an envelope, I smelled perfume and glanced up. Beth Sawyer had made it upstairs with her camera guy and was standing in front of my desk with her big blue eyes blinking.

"Let's talk about these murders you're investigating." Her diction was broadcast clear, so I checked the photographer and he wasn't shooting pictures.

"No comment." She stood next to my desk like an attractive viper, but I remembered the bad press.

"Heard you were a hero in Vietnam." I recognized a con job when I saw it coming. "Said you won medals."

"So did a lot of people," I said. "Sacks was the hero. I happened to be there."

"Aren't you worried about what's going to happen?"

"What do you mean?"

"Even as we speak, those agents from the attorney general's staff are giving their report on you to Sheriff Riggins. Doesn't that worry you?"

I shrugged. "Whatever happens will happen. When you're innocent, you don't have to chew your fingernails. How do you know that he's getting the AG's report?"

"Got my sources." She smiled.

Riggins's office door swung open, and he motioned for me to come in. I entered and closed the door behind me. The two agents got up from their chairs as I moved to the center of his office.

"They cleared you," said Riggins. I couldn't decide if he wanted to smile or cry. "They couldn't prove anything."

I looked at the taller agent, the one wearing the Stetson. "Believe your name is Ennis Maddrey?"

"You've got a good memory," he said. "Do you want the AG to put a letter of clearance in your official file?"

"Damned right I do," I snapped. "And I hope that television reporter waiting outside gets to see it. She owes me equal time."

"The AG has given me a prepared statement for the media," Maddrey said. "We can't tell them how to use it, but we hope you do get equal time. The AG himself notified the media of this meeting."

"Wish he'd told me," I said.

The two agents walked out, and Maddrey handed Beth a copy of the AG's news release.

"You mean he's innocent?" Her voice was suddenly squeaky.

"We have no evidence supporting any wrongdoing by Deputy Stark," Maddrey said.

"Shit," she said. "I came all the way from Roanoke for this." She whirled and stomped out. I smiled and listened to her heels clicking as she walked down the hall. Riggins rushed out and followed after her.

The two state agents wished me luck and marched off, each carrying a fat briefcase. I respected them for their objectivity.

When they were gone, Gloria said, "That wasn't the report Beth wanted or expected."

Riggins came back looking dejected. "She didn't want a statement from me."

"Reckon it'll be a sad day for us all when good news makes headlines," I said.

"The media can ruin you," Riggins said.

Before I could answer, the telephone buzzed and Gloria picked up. "Sheriff, it's for you. Hokie Preston is on the line."

I couldn't hear Hokie's end of the conversation, but Riggins was nodding and agreeing. When he hung up, he frowned at me. "Hokie thinks we need to search out the Huckleberry Section around Horse Heaven Mountain. I agree, but I think I should go with you to make sure it's done right. Should we find something big, it might get me back in good with Beth Sawyer."

"Probably ought to get Frosty, too," I said. "Gonna be a lot of walking if we do it right."

"Want Billy Bob and my reserves?"

"The fewer the better so we won't leave a lot of tracks."

"When are we going?" he said.

"In the morning when the frost melts. That way we won't leave signs."

"I'll put our talkies on charge." He went to a filing cabinet and removed them from a drawer.

I hoped that Riggins would be tight-lipped about our plans. The last thing I wanted was a caravan of his coffee-drinking cronies from Maggie's following us to Horse Heaven Mountain. But I had no control over that. Gloria could be trusted to keep mum.

On the way out, I stopped by the tax collector's office and picked up a county map that covered the Huckleberry Section. I folded it into my jacket pocket and took it home to study so I could learn all I could about the topography.

My place was lonely that night with Tina gone, but I heated some leftovers and finished a bottle of red wine that had been left in the refrigerator. I stacked the dirty dishes in the sink and unfolded the map on my dining room table. With scissors, I cut out the part detailing Horse Heaven Mountain, but it failed to show the abandoned mine sites. We'd have to discover them on our own. It showed Old Train Lane looping around the mountain and intersecting with Highway 21, which I already knew. With a ballpoint pen, I made an X mark where I figured Joe Sacks's cabin stood.

Before crawling into bed, I got out my walking boots, a pair of heavy socks, and an insulated hunting jacket. Then I called Tina's apartment but she didn't answer, and I hung up after six rings. I intended to call her again later but I fell asleep.

CHAPTER
Thirty-Four

Beth Sawyer was sitting on the corner of my desk when I got to the office the next morning. Her skirt was above her knees and she was showing shapely legs that would stir Frosty's imagination. Her bottled blond hair glistened, and she was made up to go on camera. She introduced her photographer, the young man who'd been with her the previous day. Gloria squinted at me but didn't say a word. I realized that Riggins had been at it again.

Without speaking, I pulled out my chair and flopped down hard. Beth chose to ignore my cold shoulder and toyed with a Styrofoam cup and sipped some coffee. After a few minutes, I rolled my chair back, got up, and stormed into Riggins's office, slamming the door behind me. He was hanging up the phone as I entered.

"Just called the *Roanoke Times*," he said. "They don't have anybody available to go with us."

"Go with us?"

"Hokie thinks we might learn something important, and I want the media along to document it. It'll help out in court. That's why I invited Beth Sawyer to come along. Can't have too much coverage."

"Anybody extra will be in the way," I said. "Besides, we might not find anything." One glance told me Riggins had dressed for the camera instead of the woods. "We're dealing with potentially dangerous people."

"You don't understand." He puckered his lips. "I need positive publicity. Offering her a chance to come along was the only way I could get back in her good graces."

"Call Hokie. Ask him about liability. She could sue us if something went wrong. Worse, she could compromise our case."

"Damn it," he said, "I'm the sheriff, not you."

"But you won't be if something tragic happens. This same media will ride you out on a rail."

"She'll sign a release—"

"Bullshit. What if we had to shoot somebody? She'd be in a position to crucify us, and she would for a big story."

"I'll make her a promise," he said.

"Let her wait at Sheppard's Store," I said. "Tell her she can come to the scene when we find something. At Sheppard's, she'll be close enough and also at a safe distance."

"She might not—"

"It's our call," I said. "Also, you'd better notify Paul Simmons. He'll be pissed if you leave him out. Come elections, you'll need his support."

Beth looked at me most unkindly when Riggins told her that she'd have to wait with Frosty at Sheppard's Store. "Didn't you promise that we could go? My producer won't like this at all."

"You won't have to wait long," Riggins said.

"You don't have to go if you don't want," I said. "Not sure we're gonna find anything worthwhile. Anyhow, you're not dressed for walking through brush."

Frosty came too late to ogle Beth's bare legs. She'd moved off my desk and was talking to her cameraman when he entered, but her presence caused him to do a double take. Before leaving, I gave Beth directions to Sheppard's and told her Frosty would join her there.

On the way to Horse Heaven Mountain, Frosty grumbled because Beth wasn't going to be his riding companion. "She could have waited with me while you and the boss walked," he said. There's no fool like an old fool, I thought.

"In case you don't hear from us," I said, "make a pass through in four hours. I'll drag some bushes into the road to show you where to stop."

"Won't be necessary," Riggins said. "We got talkies."

"Sometimes the handsets don't break the relay," I said.

Frosty stopped on Old Train Lane in the vicinity of Joe's cabin. The weather was warmer than usual for late December, about forty degrees, but a breezy north wind hinted that cooler temperatures were coming. Riggins slammed the car door loud enough to keep us from surprising anyone in that vicinity. Then he stumbled when his feet got tangled in some roots and dead vines clinging to the ground. He sounded like a bull elephant as he snorted ahead with his .44 Magnum swinging in his shoulder holster that wasn't attached to his belt.

We pushed our way deeper into the woods through brambles and fighting thorn bushes that scratched our hands. I led the way and made a path for Riggins to follow. He was breathing hard after five minutes. "Hell," he said, "we don't have to be in a big hurry."

We climbed the hillside until Joe's cabin was beneath us. I looked down through the bare hardwood trees and saw nothing to arouse my interest. Riggins was stomping heavily, and breaking sticks and crunching dried leaves. Every so often, he asked me to stop for him to catch his breath.

"You walk too damned fast," he said. He was sweating profusely, and we still had a long way to go. "I should have stayed in the car and let Frosty walk."

I shook my head. "He's in worse shape than you."

Riggins flipped out his talkie. "I'm calling him. If I can find my way back to the road, he can pick me up and you can finish by yourself. Don't look as if we gonna find anything."

Riggins pressed the button but couldn't break the relay. "Damn it," he said, "it isn't working. New battery, too."

I nodded. "This is one of those dead areas I've told you about. Remember when I asked you to get a booster relay out here?"

"So why did we bring the talkies?"

"You've got spots where they'll work," I said. "Get on top of Horse Heaven Mountain and you can talk to anybody in the county. I told Frosty to drive through in about four hours."

"But I told him not to."

"Frosty has been around long enough to know what to do if he doesn't hear from us."

Riggins faltered along about ten steps behind me, creating more pandemonium than a squadron of choppers. We made slow progress, and I had to pull him up steep inclines when we came to one. Twice he lost his footing and would have fallen if I hadn't held his arm. "I'm thirsty," he said. "Did you bring a canteen?"

I shook my head. "We'll have to find a stream."

Riggins was exhausted when I spotted what I took to be an old logging road. I didn't see any recent tracks, but somebody had bulldozed a ten-foot path up the mountain from Old Train Lane. While I inspected the road, Riggins found a tree stump, sat, and yanked out a handkerchief to wipe sweat from his face. His sagging jowls were flushed, and his lips had turned white.

"It's an old logging path." He was rasping between pants.

"Not sure it's old, and I'm not sure it's a logging path." I pointed to gravel in the roadbed. "How many loggers put a rock bottom on their roads?"

"I don't know." He had removed his hat. He was scratching his head with both hands. "Any fool can see that dual wheels like loggers use made those ruts."

"Let's backtrack," I said. "I want to see where this path originates."

"You go. I'll wait here. My legs have given out. This tree stump sits mighty good. Let me sit and rest."

I was glad to go without him because of the racket he made. I stepped quietly down the slope, walking outside the ruts so I wouldn't leave tracks. It took me at least a half hour to reach where the path intersected with Old Train Lane. Somebody had camouflaged the entrance with a log gate covered with brush and attached to a pair of heavy locust posts.

I'd driven through many times and hadn't noticed this. It was an old moonshiner trick to sweep away tracks, but I'd never seen anything like this. The underbrush behind the gate was stomped down smooth from traffic. I found a couple of discarded flashlight batteries, which told me this was a night operation.

I was careful not to leave signs that I'd been there. Then I started my trek back to where I left Riggins sitting on a tree stump. The return was a 10 percent upgrade, and I unbuttoned my jacket to cool down. When I arrived at the stump, nobody was there. But I smelled cigar smoke and figured that he was in the vicinity.

Maybe he'd stepped into the bushes to take a leak, I thought. Then a deep voice with a Northern accent that I recognized spoke. "Put your hands over your head. Make a false move, and I'll kill both you and the sheriff."

Jake Monsure, the former football pro, shoved Riggins from behind an oak tree onto the path. He was holding a large black revolver in his left hand. He pointed it at my chest. "You've been snooping around too much for your own health." He'd cuffed Riggins's hands behind him. A pencil-thin trickle of blood seeped from Riggins's nostrils. "We were expecting you because everybody in town knew you were coming. You and the black-headed bitch should have stayed out of this area. Wouldn't have found you so soon if the sheriff hadn't lit a cigar."

Riggins looked down. "Gonna get yourself in a lot of trouble if you don't let me go. I'm the high sheriff of this county."

"Shut up, old man. I'll smack you again if you say one more word." Monsure tightened his lips and looked at me. "The old fool didn't have to get himself in the middle of this."

I saw a movement behind Monsure. Hamp Stallings stepped out of the woods, brandishing a sawed-off double-barrel shotgun. He pointed it at me and cocked the hammers. Nothing looks bigger than a shotgun when you're looking down both barrels. Stallings's body was trembling. "Get your hands up like the man said." His high-pitched voice quivered.

This was no time for heroics. I raised my hands just as a third man came into view. He was heavyset, not huge like Monsure, but bigger than Stallings. His face was pockmarked under a short, dark beard. I figured he'd been the shooter in the van because he was carrying a .270 Winchester with a scope.

Monsure grinned at him. "Phillip, look what we've got here." Peering at me through slanted charcoal eyes, Phillip moved closer in my direction. His heavy eyebrows, fused in a perpetual scowl, seemed to support the bill of his woolen hunters' cap. I didn't feel that he had my best interests in his heart.

Without warning, he slugged me with the gun stock. My brain exploded into purple and crimson as the lights went out.

CHAPTER
Thirty-Five

I don't know how long I was unconscious. When I opened my eyes, I was confused by the darkness and couldn't think clearly. I smelled damp earth and thought I was back in Nam, and that Charlie had dragged me into a tunnel. I lay on my back with sharp rocks jabbing into my body. My head felt like they'd taken a power drill and bored a hole in it, and that the bit had broken off and was still revolving inside. When I tried moving my arms, I found my hands were tied behind me. My ankles were bound, too.

Then I heard groaning and figured it was Riggins. I stared in the direction of the sound. It was too dark to see anything. I smelled blood and guessed it was my own. Chemical fumes and the stink of rottenness hung heavy in the cold, clammy air.

"Where in the hell are we?" I managed to say.

"You still alive?"

"Not sure. Where are we?"

"In a cave next to an old mine shaft." Riggins's voice was weak and without his normal bluster.

"How long we been here?" I struggled to make the words come out because speaking caused pain that assaulted my head.

"Not sure," he said, "but I'd guess about an hour or so. They're waiting for their boss. Think they plan to kill us. I don't want to die this way."

"Who's their boss?"

"Didn't say. Just said he'd be here in a little while. The bastards took my gold railroad watch. It's the Hamilton my grandpap carried. Sumbitches put my own handcuffs on me, and that big sumbitch got my pearl-handled .44, too."

"I'm tied with rope or something," I said.

"Bailing twine," Riggins said. "You didn't have your cuffs on you. Watched them roll you over and tie your wrists."

"Do you know any of them?"

"Naw," he said. "Never seen them before that I can remember. I got a feeling they had something to do with killing Sacks, though. He'd been tied up with the same kind of bailing twine they used on you. I watched them search you and take your gun, wallet and keys. The one with the beard tied your hands."

"How far did they bring us?"

"Don't know," he said. "They threw us into the back of a van. Then they drove to an opening in the mountain. Looks like a big old shaft. They dumped us in a smaller hole next to the big opening and slammed the door."

"Must be the old Ganaway mine," I said. "Heard hunters talk about it, but I've never been here before."

"Frosty will figure out a way to save us," said Riggins.

"It'll be a week before he can get enough help to search. He won't even realize we're missing until dark. He'll think we got lost or something. Hope this doesn't mess up your relations with Beth Sawyer."

He didn't answer.

In about an hour, the door swung open and the shaft of light rushing in was blinding. It took my eyes several seconds to adjust. Three men entered, with Monsure leading the way. He drew a knife from his pocket and cut the bailing twine from my feet. "You're too heavy to drag." He folded the knife with his heavy hands and dropped it back into his jacket pocket. Then he and Stallings grabbed my coat and yanked me up. I almost fell.

"Don't get any ideas or I'll blow you away." I spotted the .357 in Monsure's waistband and knew that he wasn't bluffing. They marched Riggins and me into a clearing outside the cave. An invigorating breeze resurrected me, and I sucked deeply. Then I blew the stale cave air from my lungs and looked around.

They'd built a loading dock with a concrete floor and steel pilings at the mine's entrance. I saw two forklifts, one with a barrel adapter, on the platform. A green John Deere tractor with a front-end loader was on the ground parked near Stallings's flatbed in a muddy turnaround. Several barrels, some red with rust, sat bunched together next to bales wrapped in brown burlap.

I knew there had to be another entrance when I saw Stallings's flatbed trailer parked at the turnaround. The path I found leading up from Old Train Lane was too narrow to handle semis. With my peripheral vision, I saw what appeared to be a wider and more traveled road coming from the direction of Highway 21.

Monsure saw me looking and must have read my mind. "Yeah, we got another way to get here. You found our emergency road," he said and shoved me forward, causing me to stumble. Stallings pushed Riggins, and we proceeded for a few steps more and then they stopped.

I gasped in surprise when I saw Conrad DeWitte approaching, and a wave of relief swept over me until I saw the stern look in his eyes and realized he wasn't on a rescue mission. He stopped in front of us and just stared at Riggins and me with a hurt look on his face. His hair was flowing in the wind, and he had on a red twilled shirt. For the longest time he was silent, and then he shook his head. "It's a shame you boys have got yourselves into trouble," he finally said.

"Are you gonna kill us?" Panic came from Riggins. "We're lodge brothers, Conrad. Think of the times we've been hunting together. Tell these damned people to turn us loose."

"I wish I could." DeWitte frowned and was tight-lipped as he looked at us opaquely. "It's not that simple."

"We've always been buddies," Riggins said. "Let me go, and I'll never mention any of this." I noted that I wasn't included.

"No, there are others involved," DeWitte said. "By being nosy, you've forced our hand and leave us with no alternative."

"What are you into?" I said. "As lodge brothers, we might be able to help."

"It's gone too far for that." He bit his lower lip. "No way you could get us out of murder charges. I didn't pull the trigger, but I could hang for killing Joe Sacks. I must say that I didn't realize that he was a lodge brother until you told me. Thank God his dues weren't current. I did check into that with the lodge secretary."

"Why did he have to die?" Although strength was returning into my voice, my head still throbbed when I spoke.

Monsure interrupted. "He brought it on himself. I told him to stay off this land, but he got curious when he heard trucks passing his house one night. He came snooping, and I grabbed his ass before he knew what was happening. Ha, he even told me that you, Deputy Stark, would even the score if we hurt him."

"Why dump his body on the Rowan farm?" I asked.

"That was a mistake," Monsure said. "We wanted somebody to find him away from here so people wouldn't be searching around his cabin and find this place. We should've dumped his body in another county far away from your jurisdiction."

"Sacks did this county a disservice," DeWitte said. "Our operation was a multimillion-dollar business that provided the county with jobs until you spoiled it. It was a lovely deal for both industry and our community."

"What kind of deal?" I asked.

Monsure said, "We bury waste nobody else wants."

"What kind of waste?" I said.

"Spent uranium and old chemicals mostly," Monsure said. "You'd think the uranium was little pellets of lime."

DeWitte cleared his throat as a signal for Monsure to quit talking. He said, "Don't you see this stuff has to be deposited somewhere? Our regulations are so intolerable that industry is quite willing to pay a premium price for this disposal."

"Joe was killed over this?" I said.

"It was out of our control," DeWitte said.

"That's why you shot him in the chest?"

"Not me," he replied. "I don't shoot people. I help my community. Look at the widows and orphans I've rescued from starvation."

"So you're gonna let us die, too?" Riggins said.

DeWitte looked away and didn't answer.

"You've got a trucking company and a logging operation. Why get mixed up in this?" I asked.

"Blame deregulation," he said. "The big haulers cut their shipping rates, and I couldn't make it with Roadway, Yellow, and Consolidated getting the cream of the freight business. My logging operations couldn't support everything, and a lot of people were going to be without jobs unless I took action."

"How did you discover this old mine?" Riggins asked.

"I was fortunate," he said. "A certain United States senator and I bought this mountain with the idea of selling it to the National Forest Service. That's when we discovered the mine and thought it would be profitable to handle refuse. The senator was pressuring the Forest Service to buy and I had to slow him down. We could make more money in the garbage business than we ever could from selling the land. The senator got the purchase delayed five or six years, but he had no part in this operation, except to share the profits."

"Is toxic stuff in those barrels?" I said.

"Probably. We don't ask many questions. Whatever it is, it'll be safe underground. This is far enough from town not to threaten anybody's health."

"You used Toby Martin as a decoy when things got hot," I said.

He nodded. "Didn't want you looking around Sacks's cabin, which happens to be on our land. Jake and Phillip searched it to make sure he hadn't left you any notes or messages. By supplying you information, I was able to keep up with the investigation. But Martin wasn't innocent. He needed to be investigated."

"Somebody is gonna find out eventually," I said.

"You're wrong," he said and walked off.

Monsure pushed Riggins and me back to the mine entrance. "You and this shithead of a sheriff are gonna be buried below, soon as Hamp fetches our plastics. We're having an implosion, and this mine will cave in."

"What's an implosion?" Riggins said.

I frowned. "He'll shape C-4 compound into cones and direct their force inward. It's the opposite of an explosion."

"You're smarter than I thought," Monsure said. "Do you know you're making us move our business to a site in Tennessee?"

I didn't have a reply, so I thought for a moment and then asked him why they objected to Tina Jordan taking water samples.

"Dead fish floating in the streams below suggested a leachate problem, but only a few people live out here," he said. "When the boss voted for her survey, he didn't know it included Horse Heaven Mountain. Thought she'd be mostly around Burnsville, where the population is centered."

"You can't do this—" began Riggins.

"Yes, I can," Monsure interrupted. "But I'll get the boss to ask them to pray for you in church."

"Sumbitch," Riggins muttered.

"Stallings will be here in a minute," Monsure said. "We'll take you back down the mine shaft for the end. You won't have any more worries. No income tax forms to fill out, no bills to pay, no nothing."

I tugged at my wrists, but the knot just got tighter. Riggins looked down. Tears gathered in his eyes.

"How did you meet DeWitte?" I said to Monsure.

"Me and the senator," he said. "We're old-time friends. I was his bodyguard after my football career ended."

"How did DeWitte hook up with the senator?"

"He was a big contributor a few years back when the senator tried to run for president."

Then I knew the name of the senator—John Edward Wellington—war hero and advocate for popular causes. Except for a sex scandal, he might have become president.

At that moment, Stallings showed up carrying a large cloth satchel heavy enough to tilt him when he walked. He smiled wickedly, unzipped the bag, pulled out a plastic packet of C-4 compound, and waved it. "At least my hitch in the National Guard taught me something."

"Got everything you need?" Monsure said.

Stallings shook his head. "More to get—want it all to go in one big shot."

"When you get what you need, take the forklift and move that stuff on the dock inside. Then we'll load the equipment on the flatbed. Nothing is to be left outside."

Stallings went away again. I wanted to grab his straw-colored ponytail and slam his face into a tree. He walked slowly, and I was glad. I wasn't in a hurry to die.

When he reappeared, he was toting a spool of white primacord that I figured he'd stolen from the Guard. He set it on the ground and wiped his forehead. He dug into the bottom of the bag and pulled out crimpers for securing the blasting cap on the fuse. The cap would set off the primacord and ignite the C-4 packets simultaneously.

Monsure turned toward Phillip. "You guard them. I'll be checking to be sure we don't have more trespassers. When Hamp is ready, you can dump them with the rest of the garbage." For someone so huge, Monsure had an agile stride. I could picture him tearing through a defensive line.

Stallings was busy squeezing the doughlike C-4 into cone shapes. He was warming it with his hands so it'd be easier to mash. He took a box of safety caps from his pocket and laid them on top of the primacord. Then he stood. "I'm gonna start the generator so we'll have light in the mine," he told Phillip.

Phillip prodded me in the ribs with the barrel of his rifle. "You got a hard head. I thought I hit you harder than that." He snickered, flashing uneven yellow teeth. "They wouldn't let me shoot you like I wanted. I'm good with a rifle. Used to work at a feed mill killing rats."

"Please let me go," Riggins said. "Let me go, and I'll forget we ever saw anything. I've got a wife and grandchildren."

"Just shut up," Phillip said.

CHAPTER
Thirty-Six

They marched us onto the loading platform and with rough hands propelled us forward, causing us to stagger across the cement deck. Stallings pulled open a heavy wooden double door at the mine portal. Phillip stopped us briefly while Stallings fired up the engine of the forklift equipped with the barrel adapter.

When I saw the darkened shaft leading into the mine, I resisted the claustrophobia that threatened to make me panic. Caves had always terrified me, and I was glad that I'd been too big for tunnel-rat duty in Nam. In my present situation, I couldn't fight back with my hands tied behind me. I saw that Riggins was handling his fright by mumbling, "Sumbitch . . . "

"Gonna let the forklift warm up first so it won't stall," Stallings told Phillip, who jostled me forward. Riggins hesitated, but Phillip slapped his face. My feet slipped on furrows of wet loam churned up by forklift traffic. Dim reflections from the overhead lights framed the narrow gangway ahead, showing seepage oozing from its rocky walls.

A hundred years before, the miners had used iron picks and mules with drag pans to excavate the shaft. They'd left their scars on the walls and bucket-sized clumps of iron ore on the floor. Phillip stopped us at the entrance of a large opening with an underground stream flowing through. The room was better lighted than the passageway, and I could see that it was braced with overhead timbers. Two dozen big lightbulbs dangled from wiring strung across the exposed crossbeams.

Without warning, Phillip hit me between the shoulders with his rifle butt, and I fell forward, landing on my

stomach. Then he secured my feet again. Stallings pushed
Riggins, causing him to fall across the top of my body and
roll off. He lay still and didn't move. I heard him moan and
figured that he was conscious. As Phillip tied Riggins's
feet, Stallings fished a roach from his shirt pocket and
flicked his lighter. Its sickly sweet odor didn't smell as bad
as the garbage around us. "Soon as I do my joint, we'll
show you real excitement. Don't even think about escaping
because you can't. If you make us shoot, you'll die slow
and painful. Besides, you'd miss the fireworks."

"Can't blow anything yet," Phillip told Stallings. "You
gotta clear the loading dock first." I thought I detected a
Midwestern accent in his voice, but I wasn't sure. "Don't
get your ass high on that weed. You got work to do. And
leave off that damned crystal. It fucks up your mind."

For a man who didn't drink, I thought, Stallings surely
had surprising vices. Marijuana might give him a buzz, but
angel dust would blow away his brain.

"Don't worry about me," Stallings said. "The forklift
can get all that stuff down here in no time. I'll bring the
barrels first and then get the bales." He walked off and
disappeared going up the tunnel. I heard his feet sloshing
in the muck.

Phillip leaned against a rock ledge, pointing the .270 at
us. "It'd be easier to shoot you," he said. "If it was up to
me, I would. For some reason, the boss wants you blown
up and buried when these walls come tumbling down. One
blast and those supporting beams are gone."

I lay there playing possum, desperate for a chance to
break free. My head throbbed, but my brain was busily
looking for an avenue of escape. With my hands tied, it was
going to be hard, and I knew Riggins would be useless as
tits on a boar hog.

The forklift was returning. I heard Stallings rev the
engine, and its putt-putt grew louder as he neared, filling
the air with carbon monoxide. He was coming fast, and
then I heard a crash. A barrel descended the gangway,
rolling wildly into the opening, barely missing me. It

banged into other barrels, knocking a couple splashing into the underground stream. I looked toward the tunnel but couldn't see what had happened. But I did hear a flurry of cuss words.

"Forklift got away from me," Stallings yelled to Phillip. He didn't have his shotgun and was busy slapping mud from his corduroy trousers. "It's overturned and I can't get it upright by myself. Untie those bastards so they can help turn it back over."

Phillip handed him the .270. He removed a knife from his pocket and frowned at Stallings. "Sure you didn't do crystal? You're acting goofy."

"Just cut them loose." Stallings's words had an exaggerated speed. "That barrel may have busted when it rolled. Something is burning my nose."

For a second time, the bailing twine was clipped from my ankles. Phillip jerked me to my feet and whacked my wrists free. "Shoot him if tries anything," he told Stallings, who was laughing crazily and waving the .270 from Riggins to me. Phillip stooped and cut the twine from Riggins's feet. "Damn," he said, "don't have the key to these cuffs."

"Hell," Stallings said, "Jake gave it to me. Here it is." He dug into his jacket pocket and fished it out. "Uncuff that old windbag of a sheriff." Stallings moved in close as he handed the key to Phillip, who was lifting Riggins to his feet. I knew this was my only chance, so I readied myself to pounce. Stallings held the rifle loosely while Phillip was unlocking the cuffs.

I kicked the gun with my right foot and sent it spinning into the burlap bales several feet away. Then I quickly caught Stallings with a straight right that smashed the bridge of his nose. I felt the impact all the way to my shoulder and knew I'd broken bones.

As he reeled backwards, I grabbed Phillip's shoulder with my left hand and spun him around. Then I brought my right forearm under his chin and locked him in a choke hold with my left hand. He was strong and struggled to break free. I held tight for dear life and used all of my strength to crush his larynx. When he'd ceased breathing, I let his collapsed body slump into a heap. His glassy eyes reflected the overhead lights.

I turned but Stallings had hightailed it. Riggins was sitting on his haunches, but I hoisted him to his feet. Luckily, Phillip had left the key in the cuffs. "We've got to get our asses out of here," I said as I uncuffed him. Fumes from the leaking barrel were stinging my nose and the atmosphere was chokedamp. I moved Riggins forward, hoping that we could get out before Stallings set off his blast.

Next to the overturned forklift, I found Stallings's double-barrel shotgun on the ground. I picked it up and broke open the breach, and saw that it held two unfired shells. If Monsure waited ahead, I knew that I'd need it. So I stuffed the gun under my arm and continued pressing Riggins forward.

"Keep moving," I said. "If he cuts off the lights, we'll never find our way out of here."

"Sumbitch . . . ," Riggins muttered.

Seconds later we caught up with Stallings, who was floundering as he staggered up the tunnel. He'd cupped both hands over his face trying to stop the blood from gushing out of his nose. I handed the shotgun to Riggins, who squeezed it against his chest and stared blankly ahead. I caught up with Stallings and tapped him on the shoulder. He hadn't heard me and looked startled.

"You're under arrest." I slammed him against the side of the shaft, turned him around, and double-locked his wrists in Riggins's handcuffs. "I'm charging you with murder, and don't make a statement because I don't have time to advise you of your rights."

His mouth twisted but nothing came out. My punch had laid his nose sideways. "I didn't kill anybody," he finally said.

"Told you not to say anything," I said. "You're gonna need a lawyer."

"Who did I kill? I'm innocent."

I nodded. "Yes, you're innocent. You're guilty of Phillip's death. By helping him commit a felony, you were responsible for making me strangle him."

"That's not fair."

"It's the law," I said. "You better think about working yourself a deal with the commonwealth attorney. Else, it's the electric chair. He might trade you the hot seat for some testimony."

He didn't reply but was coughing up and spitting blood he'd swallowed. "My eyes are swelling and I'm bleeding to death," he said.

Riggins clawed his way to where I held Stallings and handed me the shotgun. "If you see that big sumbitch, shoot him on sight and get my pearl-handled .44 back."

Once I led Riggins and Stallings outside, it took a minute for my eyes to adjust to natural light. I didn't see Monsure, so I held the shotgun like a barbell and pressed it over my head several times to restore circulation. At that moment, I was glad I didn't have to do battle with Monsure. He'd moved like a ringer and he wouldn't be easy at all. His kind needed to be shot on sight. The black van was gone, and I figured Monsure had left in it. Riggins rubbed his sore nose with the back of his hand and glanced at Stallings. His wormy lips quivered, and his drooping jowls almost touched his collar. "You're in big trouble," he told Stallings. "You forgot that I'm the high sheriff of this county."

"Where're our handsets?" I said to Stallings.

"Jake took them. Guess he's got them in the van."

"How were you and Phillip getting away from here?" I said.

"In the flatbed," he said. "I was gonna take it to our headquarters in Burnsville. The keys are in the switch."

"Let's go to Sheppard's and get Frosty," Riggins said.

"We'd better go straight to town," I said. "We can radio Frosty from there, and this man does need the emergency room. Besides, I don't want to see Beth Sawyer and her photographer right now, and you're not dressed to go on camera. Look at your hair."

"To hell with my hair. Look at this blood on my new shirt. Can you drive that truck?" he asked.

"We'll see," I said. "I'm gonna let Stallings start the engine, and after I cuff him again, I'm heading for town."

My first shot at operating a ten-speed tractor hooked to a forty-eight-foot trailer would have been less challenging had I understood the transmission. I scraped the gears until I got the hang of double-clutching. I glanced through the big Hollywood mirrors hanging on the cab and didn't see anyone following, so I figured we had a straight shot into town.

When I turned my first corner in Burnsville, I didn't swing wide enough and uprooted a fire hydrant that left water spurting skyward. "So much for town-county relations," I told Riggins.

"Shoot that sumbitch who got my pearl-handled pistol," he replied.

I knew then I wasn't skilled enough to maneuver the rig into the hospital parking area, and I drove toward the courthouse. Stallings would have to wait for his trip to the ER.

Two blocks down the main drag, I heard a siren and saw flashing blue lights. A town police cruiser was racing up behind me. I hit the air brakes, and the big rig bounced to a stop. Officer Leonard Wren, the rookie who was about to give the Red Bullet a parking ticket, vaulted from the car. He approached with his citation book already out.

"Put away your tickets and get us some help," I said. "We've got an injured prisoner on our hands."

Riggins jumped out of the cab. "I need to go to the hospital, too," he said. "I'll help escort Stallings." Wren used the mutual aid channel on his cruiser to radio Frosty and have him meet me at the courthouse.

For once I found Gloria out of her chair and pacing the floor when I walked into the office. "My God," she said.

"You look like you've been in a wreck. Your head is caked with blood. You need medical attention."

"Don't have time," I said. "Unlock the safe because I'm checking out a spare service revolver."

CHAPTER
Thirty-Seven

When Hokie met me a few minutes later at the sheriff's office, he looked at my banged-up head and gasped. "Did you get hit by a train?"

"No, but it felt like it," I said. "I'm charging Conrad DeWitte and his assistant, Jake Monsure, with the murder of Joe Sacks, and I hope they rot in hell. A third defendant is being treated for a broken nose at the hospital."

Hokie was stunned. "Are you out of your mind? Do you realize DeWitte has more political pull than anyone in the county?"

"Don't care about his pull. He's got a huge toxic waste dump on Horse Heaven Mountain, and his people killed Sacks to protect it. Will you help me word the affidavit?"

Hokie shrugged. "Doesn't look like I have a choice. I just hope you know what you're doing and that bump on your head hasn't affected your thinking."

After he scribbled on a yellow legal pad, we walked across the street to the magistrate's office. He dictated a complaint while the magistrate prepared conspiracy warrants charging DeWitte, Monsure, and Stallings with murder. I placed my left hand on the Bible and raised my right hand, swearing that what Hokie had dictated was true to the best of my knowledge.

The magistrate handed me the warrants, and I stepped outside to find Frosty, Billy Bob, and Wren waiting. "It's time to kick ass," Frosty said. "Billy Bob and Leonard want in on the action, too."

"Where's Beth and her news crew?" I asked.

"I ditched them when Wren radioed me to get my ass back here."

Just before sunset, the four of us went in two cars to
DeWitte's office building. The lot was vacant except for the
black van and a scattering of vehicles randomly parked
about the premises.

"They kept Riggins in the hospital," Wren said. "He
was complaining of chest pains, and the ER folks thought
he'd better spend the night."

I directed him and Billy Bob to cover the rear of the
building. "Don't take any chances because these people are
dangerous and desperate."

Frosty went with me to the front entrance, which was
unlocked, and we pushed through the glass doors. The
fiery-haired receptionist had gone for the day, so we started
down the corridor toward DeWitte's private office.

As we rounded a corner, I came face-to-face with
Monsure. He tried to grab me in his arms, but I blocked his
move by bringing my forearms sharply upward. I aimed a
kick at his groin, but he turned sideways, taking the blow
on his thigh. Before he could hit me, Frosty diverted his
attention by rushing forward with a drawn pistol. Monsure
slapped the gun away and booted Frosty in the chest,
sending him backwards to the floor. I slugged him between
the eyes. To my alarm, the punch brought a smile to his
face. Then, he charged.

I sidestepped his rush and struck him between the
shoulders when he passed. His momentum carried him
into the wall. Before I could follow through, he quickly
spun around and swung a roundhouse right that I was
lucky enough to duck. His fist zoomed past my head and
smashed loudly into the plaster wall behind me. The
impact brought a scream, but it didn't stop him. He kicked
and I dodged it, but he landed a glancing left hook on my
jaw. His pain seemed to make him fight harder. He blocked
a kick with his sore hand, but the contact made him wince.

I opened up with a flurry of punches, throwing
everything I had. He fought back with his left fist. One lick
grazed the top of my head and reopened my wound,
causing it to bleed.

I kicked him on the shin as he moved forward and seized me in a bear hug that was robbing me of breath. I grabbed his ear and yanked downward. It almost came off in my hand. Blood spurted, and he momentarily relaxed his grip. I gouged his eye with my thumb and it popped out of its socket. He grabbed me again and I thrust my wounded head upward, smashing his face. I gouged his other eye and kneed him where it hurt. He bent forward, and I let go with a front thrust kick that caught him in the belly.

As he was falling, I said, "That was for Joe Sacks." Then I kicked him again in the ribs and told him that one was for Joe's dog.

Frosty had managed to get to his feet, pick up his pistol, and point it at Monsure as he rolled on the hallway floor. "Freeze or I shoot."

Monsure lay moaning with his hands cupped around his groin.

"Where's DeWitte?" I said.

A mixture of slobber and blood pooled on the floor beneath his face. He didn't answer. Frosty and I rolled him over and cuffed his hands behind him. Monsure tried to speak, but all I heard were mumbles.

"Go get DeWitte," Frosty said. "I'll guard this guy, and if he looks at me wrong he's a dead man."

I climbed the short flight of stairs and stopped for a moment at the door to DeWitte's private office before kicking it open.

He was calmly sitting in his swivel chair holding Riggins's talkie. "Been expecting you," he said. "Believe it or not, I'm really glad you weren't killed. Always thought you and Riggins were good men."

"You're under arrest," I said, "for murder, conspiracy to commit murder, and some charges I can't even pronounce."

"Oh, my."

He leaned back and stared at the ceiling as I Mirandized him. I yanked him to his feet, and he offered no resistance as I locked the cuffs.

Monsure had gone into shock, and Billy Bob and Wren took him to the hospital, while Frosty and I conducted DeWitte eastward to the courthouse. A crowd had gathered outside, and Beth Sawyer's TV cameraman blinded us with lights as we marched DeWitte to the elevator.

Beth rushed behind us carrying a mike and asking for a statement, but I pushed DeWitte into the elevator and closed the door.

"Monsure won't testify against me, " DeWitte said. "Neither will Phillip."

"Phillip's dead," I said.

"Didn't know that," he said. "Without witnesses, you can't make murder charges stick."

I didn't tell him that Stallings would deal to save his ass. Under the rules of discovery, his lawyer would find that out in due time.

I checked my revolver with the jailer and took DeWitte to his cell across from the drunk tank. As I locked the door, I said, "Doesn't look like you're gonna be grand master next year, does it?"

CHAPTER
Thirty-Eight

Much to my annoyance, the ER folks decided to keep me overnight when Frosty drove me to the hospital. I didn't protest too much because I was exhausted and just wanted to rest. Doc Lee stopped by and said he couldn't help just yet because he only worked with the deceased. I told him his sense of humor was killing me. Riggins was in the next room, and before I drifted into a deep sleep I heard him mumbling ". . . sumbitch . . ."

The X-rays showed that my skull was intact, and they released me the next morning. To my surprise, Tina was there to pick me up.

"I got here last night," she said, "but they wouldn't let me see you."

On the way to my place, she said, "I've already put the makings for breakfast in your refrigerator. You're going to need to rest and take it easy for awhile."

I saw that she'd cleaned up the trailer and I wanted to say thanks, but my pain medicine made me drowsy and I fell asleep on the sofa. Tina woke me at eleven the next morning and told me it was time for brunch.

My head was throbbing, and I swallowed two more pills and chased them with black coffee. The food helped, and my head was clearing up enough to think. I reached out and patted her hand.

"I don't know exactly how to tell you something." She was toying with her coffee mug.

"What?" I chewed a piece of crisp bacon.

"I'm moving back to New York."

"New York?" I stopped chewing.

"Lamar called. He wants us to try again. This time he says he's putting me first and not his art shows. It's not that I don't care for you, because I do."

"Follow your heart," I said.

"I don't want to hurt you."

"We've had a special relationship."

"You're not angry?"

"Maybe hurting, but not angry." And then I tried to be magnanimous. "If you can patch it up with your ex, it might work out."

"I'm going to do my best," she said.

"How about your research here?"

"It'll continue in the next fiscal year with someone else doing it."

"Whoever they send won't be as pretty as you."

Her eyes filled, and she planted a wet kiss on my forehead.

When I returned to the office, I grimaced at the overdue paperwork cluttering my desk. I sat at my desk and began flipping through it when Gloria put down her crossword and said, "You've been promoted to detective. The sheriff has hired Leonard Wren to work your district. He tried to reach you at home, but your phone must've been unplugged."